DESIRE

CHUNICHI

STREET CHRONICLES

Copyright © 2013 Chunichi

Published by:

G Street Chronicles
P.O. Box 1822
Jonesboro, GA 30237-1822

www.gstreetchronicles.com
fans@gstreetchronicles.com

Cover design:
Hot Book Covers, www.hotbookcovers.com

ISBN13: 9781938442896
ISBN10: 193844289X
LCCN: 2013956041

Join us on our social networks

Like us on Facebook: G Street Chronicles
Follow us on Twitter: @GStreetChronicl
Follow us on Instagram: gstreetchronicles

This book is dedicated to my great niece,
Alaya Chyanne Slade.
She brings me joy each and every day.
Auntie loves you, Laya Pooka.

Prologue

" **A**aaahhhh shit! Suck it, baby. Suck this dick for daddy." Bishop whispered while gripping a handful of the silky Indian hair weave Desire wore down her back.

He forced her face deep between his legs making sure she kept pace with the up and down motion he so loved. Every once in a while, he forced it too deep, causing her to gag. Part of him felt the need to apologize for getting lost in the moment and causing her discomfort, but another part said run with the pending orgasm from her deep-throat action. Desire was impressed by the long snake that hung between his legs. Big dicks were her weakness. The lyrics of William McDowell filled the church as the choir sang in the background.

"I give myself away. I give myself away, so you can use me," the church sang.

Funny how those words were so true. Desire had given herself away to many men time and time again. Although they may have thought they were using her, in her eyes it was an even exchange. They got what they wanted and she did as well. Sometimes she even ended up with the better end of the stick.

The average woman would have felt guilty for giving the bishop head…in the house of God…during Thanksgiving service, but not Desire. She sucked the skin off his dick, like she had discovered a way of sucking out his soul. She did this all while keeping her eyes fixated on the church offering baskets that sat stacked on top of each other in the corner of the bishops office. In her head she tried to estimate how much the church had collected during the early morning service.

The debt-free fund, tithes, offering and the church 20th anniversary offering…there has to be at least $500,000 in there, Desire thought.

Eager to get this sexcaped over and money in her pocket, Desire threw things into fifth gear. She looked up at the bishop with her big hazel eyes and gave him a seductive look; she was a pro at finishing the job.

"Cum for me daddy. Cum all over my face," she whispered, then spat on his penis and gave it a few long, strong strokes, focusing on the tip of the head just the way most men liked it.

"Sinful Sunday"

Diamond Diva
SERIES

G STREET CHRONICLES
A LITERARY POWERHOUSE
WWW.GSTREETCHRONICLES.COM

Chapter 1

Desire

When Desire was locked up, she vowed to come home and live life on the straight and narrow. She sat in her jail cell day after day talking that "jail talk" with her cell mate, Isis.

Isis and Desire both came from a life of ghetto fame and fast money. It was that lifestyle that landed them in jail. Isis was doing time for some petty dope charge she took for her man, Vada. Authorities wanted Isis to snitch on her man, but she refused. He was an up and coming rap artist at the time and she didn't want to ruin his career. So when she didn't cooperate and roll over on him, they stuck her with a small possession's charge. She didn't like it but agreed to take the rap for her man. Isis was a true ride or die chick!

Isis was a lot like Desire, living in the lap of luxury as a dangerous diva. Both knew the rules of the game. They were tight as glue while they were locked up and they both swore they would never get caught up in the mix again. They weren't going to let money and material things control their lives anymore; and they meant it when they said it.

It was Isis who persuaded Desire to get involved in church, praying and reading the Bible. And at the time, it all worked. Desire was ready to turn over a new leave and was actually convinced that she was no longer pressed about designer labels, five-hundred-dollar weaves, and big whips. She was living for God, and as such she recognized that money was the root of all evil. However, it wasn't long before she began to miss the shopping sprees, American Express Black Card, the BMW X6 and having any and everything she wanted in the palms of her hands.

Isis and Desire had come up with a business plan to open a high-end salon and spa, offering a range of services from hair, nails, massages, facials and lashes to complete makeovers. It would be a woman's one-stop beauty shop, turning the drab to fab! Isis and Desire both knew this shop would be a guaranteed success. There was none like it in their area. They were determined to provide the best stylist, nail technicians, massage therapist and estheticians the city had to offer, a sure way to kill all competition.

Vada provided Isis with an attorney from the best law firm in the city. It wasn't long before his efforts paid off. After numerous court dates Isis was finally released. Although Desire was happy for her friend she was sad to see her go. Desire still had another year of time left to serve. For the first few months Desire spoke to Isis on a weekly basis. She even put money a steady flow of money on her books. After a while the money slowed down and she started accepting less of Desires phone calls. Shortly after that, everything completely stopped. Desire wasn't surprised though, she'd been locked up long enough to know what to expect. Besides, by that point she was short time so she had no worries.

When Desire was released, she was determined to get things in motion just as she and her cell mate had planned. She constantly thought about Isis as she took the steps towards their goal. This was their dream and her bestie was supposed to right by her side each step of the way, yet she was alone. Never the less, Desire put an honest effort into getting an investor and a small business loan to put their dream in action. With her credit score not being up to par and lurking under a six hundred score, and with no collateral in sight, banks were denying her repeatedly even for a small ten thousand dollar business loan. She felt discouraged, stressed out and alone. Desire desperately needed a second chance. Most lenders strongly suggested that she needed to reestablish her credit first before trying to get a loan. And it took money to do that—money she didn't have.

Feeling defeated, Desire decided to take refuge in her bedroom. Her room was the only privacy she had since she was now living with her parents. Her loft apartment overlooking the skyline of Uptown Charlotte was long gone. It was a mere faded memory now, like everything else in her life, it had been taken away from her while she was in a jail cell. Desire thoughts drifted back to the day of her arrest.

* * * * *

Ding Dong...the doorbell rang at one of the homes Desire shared with her boyfriend, King. Although the extravagant four bedroom home in the Ballantyne area of

Charlotte was funded by drug money from King, the deed and all utilities listed Desire's name. It was her pristine credit in combination with Kings money that made it possible for them to have a house, condo, and expensive cars.

Without hesitation or even glancing at the security cameras, Desire rose from her oversized sofa and headed to the front door. She opened the door to see a balding white man dressed in wrangler jeans, work boots and a tight white tee-shirt.

"Hello, I'm Detective Sherman with Mecklenburg Gang and Narcotics Unit." He flashed a badge in front of Desires face then two additional people walked up.

"Okay. So, how can I help you Detective Sherman with Mecklenburg Gang and Narcotics Unit," Desire said while looking him in the eye. She didn't budge. She stood before him fearlessly.

"This is U.S. Marshall—"

"U.S. Marshall Smith," the man beside Detective Sherman interjected. "I'm looking for Johnathan Paisley." He called King by his government name.

"In reference to what?" she asked then glanced at the other man that wore a shirt and ball cap that read ICE. She knew ICE stood for Immigration and Customs Enforcement. King was Jamaican and things weren't looking good for him at that moment.

"In reference to a federal matter. We need to take look in your home," the U.S. Marshall stated then stepped forward.

Desire pushed the door forward, slightly closing it, "No you may not."

"Ma'am, please. It will only take a moment. We just need

to make sure Mr. Paisley is not in the home." The detective said, trying to play good cop.

"This is not Mr. Paisley's home," Desire spat.

"All we need is five minutes of your time and we will not bother you again," he pleaded.

"Fine," Desire agreed then opened the door allowing them to enter.

She wasn't sure what was going on, but she knew King wasn't there or even in town at the time so they were not going to find him. She figured if she just let them in and they see that King wasn't there, they would go away and that would give her time to contact him and give him the heads up on the situation. As they looked around the house for King, Desire sat on the couch, crossed her legs and sipped on a glass of wine just as she was doing before they arrived. Five minutes later the three of them returned.

"Ma'am, is this your home or Mr. Paisley's home," the detective asked.

"As I stated earlier, this is my home. I haven't seen Mr. Paisley in months." Desire lied in an attempt to protect King.

"Okay. So it's safe to say this marijuana belongs to you," Detective Sherman said while holding up a quarter pound of weed.

At that moment, Desire felt as though her heart had stopped. Everything from that point was a complete blur.

* * * * *

Thinking back to that day made Desire sick to her stomach, but it also gave her motivation. Feeling the pressure of having to make something happen in her life stacked up high on her shoulders; and limited by the confinements of house arrest, Desire decided to turn to the internet. First she tried searching for her old cell mate, Isis. She started by doing a reverse search using her old phone number. That brought back nothing. Then she turned to social networks, giving Facebook a try. Still she got nothing. As a final attempt she did a Google search using Isis's full name.

"Wha-la"! Like magic she turned up.

When Desire hit the link she was disappointed to see nothing more than a mug shot. That was useless. Realizing her search was leading her nowhere, she directed her attention back to business. She started researching online investors and small business grants. She figured, *what's the worst they could say, "We will get back to you?"*

After two hours of researching, she was tired and was just about to give up when an advertisement popped up from a sexual website. At first glance Desire was going to delete the image, but against her better judgment, she decided to click on it. As she read over the website, Desire realized it solicited sex videos and paid for submissions. The site indicated that if she registered with their company, she could get paid each time someone viewed her video. Within an instant, Desire thought about all the money she could make with very little effort on her part. In her heart, she truly desired to be Christ-like and she wanted to earn her living the right way. But the walls were closing in on her and she needed to do something about it and fast. So Desire followed the instructions on the website and registered. Then she removed her T-shirt, her lint ball covered bra, her jeans and worn out panties and changed into her best black lace La Perla set with a matching garter belt. Being sexy was her expertise; so to add a little spice to the pot, she pulled out an old whip she had in the back of the closet. Desire set up an old apple notebook that was given to her by her mom and she recorded her version of a dominatrix good time.

"Welcome to the terror dome. My name is Danger," she said before popping her whip.

She crawled across the bed like a black cat. Then, slowly, she took off her panties, rubbed her ass, and spanked it with her left hand and then the whip.

"Hmm," she purred after taking two fingers and rubbing her clit, eventually cumming on herself. Before turning the computer off, she kissed the screen.

"I will see you tomorrow," she said smiling.

Desire woke up the next morning eager to check the status of her views. She took a deep breath hoping that someone had viewed her video and responded.

"OMG!" she shouted.

Desire had received over eleven hundred views, which equated to eleven hundred dollars from the site. She quickly started scrolling down all of the hits and comments that were left for her to view. A few men and even women had watched her video several times. One man in particular stood out. He'd watched the video ten times and requested Desire webcam with him for a personal session. Originally she had only registered for the limited service package that only allowed her to post videos. But after seeing this guy's request she decided to register for the platinum package which allowed her to have personal sessions with clients and charge by the minute. Ten minutes later she received a notification of the change on her laptop and a message from Mr. X—ready for his personal session. She immediately logged on and the picture popped up.

"Welcome to the terror dome. My name is Danger," she said then popped her whip.

Mr. X was very discrete. His face was covered with a baseball cap. His room was slightly dark and behind him sat a small table with a dim lamp and a framed photo. Eager to know who this mystery man was, Desire zoomed in on the photo. She instantly noticed a familiar face. It was none other than Bishop Sylvester Rollins of the Baptist Temple Church. Dollar signs rolled into her head like a slot machine on all 7's. Her brain went into overdrive and the old Desire was back!

Bishop Rollins had a flock of over ten thousand members who look up to him for spiritual guidance and wisdom. Desire began to question if Christian faith was even real or just a joke. She had to wonder, *if the bishop traffics sexual cam websites, what does that say about his congregation as a whole?* It was at that point Desire decided his church, Baptist Temple Church, was going to be her personal playground. She couldn't wait for Sunday to arrive so that she could pay the bishop a little visit. However, right now it was time for Danger, Bishop Rollins, her whip and the webcam.

* * * * *

When Sunday rolled around, Desire put on her Sunday best and headed to Baptist Temple. She showed up thirty minutes before the second service was scheduled to begin.

"Good morning, sister," an usher greeted with a smile while handing her a program for the service.

"Good morning," she replied taking a deep breath hoping not to be noticed.

Desire couldn't help but to glance at the stained glass windows on each side of the church and the many wooden rows. On the back of each row was a built-in book shelf that held bibles and had a holder for a communion cup. She felt a sense of history richness and the many generations before her who walked through those doors. The building was old; however, it had been kept up.

Desire wasn't there to do the Lord's work, hear the Word of Jesus or sing the selected hymns. All she wanted was to lay down her heavy burden of getting the money she earned and was owed by the bishop. As she entered into the sanctuary, the choir was singing Hezekiah Walker's song entitled, *You're All I Need*. There were only a few people in the sanctuary taking their seats. Two women were running around the church with their shoes off. Desire just figured the Holy Spirit came upon them as her mother use to say to her as a young girl. The vibe felt similar to the church she attended when she was younger. Pretending to head to the bathroom, she searched for the bishop's office. Lucky for her, it was easy to find. Boldly, she walked straight in as though she had been invited. The bishop turned white as a ghost when he saw her. He stopped talking to the men in his office mid-sentence. From what she could gather, they were discussing his sermon for the morning.

Hypocrite, she thought and shook her head in disgust.

"Brother Timon and Brother Carver, would you excuse me please? I need to speak with this young lady," Bishop Rollins instructed the men that stood before him. Without a word they exited his office.

"How may I help you?" he asked Desire with small beads of sweat developing on his forehead.

She walked closer to his desk and eventually over to his chair. Pulling up her dress, she revealed the black garter belt he had viewed on their webcam session the previous week.

"Look, I don't need any trouble. What do you want?" he asked.

"I don't want any trouble either," she said after getting down on her knees, unzipping his pants and pulling out his dick.

Giving bishop head, Karrine Steffans' style...it was time she got this over with. Desire gave him a few more strokes, took it to a deep throat and it was over.

"Hmm," he softly moaned. Sweat began to pour down his face.

She made him cum so hard it damn near paralyzed him for a few minutes. The bishop took a deep breath and closed his eyes with his hands clinched on his desk. Desire removed the handkerchief from his outer suit pocket and used it to wipe down his dick. He carefully watched her as she placed his dick back into his boxers and slowly zipped his pants back up.

"Now, Bishop, let's talk money. I need a quaint donation of five thousand dollars, that's all," she stated, reaching over him to reveal her cleavage.

"Miss, I can't take money from the church," he explained.

"I don't care where you get it from. I need it." There was a bit of commotion in the hall and the deacons came back into the office to escort the bishop to the pulpit.

"Duty calls, sister. God bless you," he said smiling, relieved that the men had rescued him.

Although Desire was fuming inside, she managed to maintain her composure. The dollar signs in her eyes had just turned to flames. She wanted to take the vase from the table and knock the bishop across the head with it. However, she knew that behavior wouldn't get her what she truly craved, so she let him have his victory. Giving a bishop a blow job wasn't the wildest thing Desire had ever done, but it was definitely the worse—at least morally speaking. She knew her actions had just purchased herself a one-way ticket straight to hell. She wasn't too concerned though, after all, as they say, "The devil wears Prada!" She was all about designer labels and would do all sorts of mischief to get it, so in this case, Desire and the Devil had a lot in common. The craziest thing was that Desire never wanted any of this. She hadn't been the one who initiated the temptation between them; the bishop had propositioned her. He'd won that battle, but not the war.

"Round one goes to you, bishop," Desire said quietly as she walked away.

Now at the pulpit, the bishop straightened his tie as he sat next to his wife, Angel. In the back of his mind he wondered if Angel noticed that he was a bit late for service. As much as he had cheated on her you would think that he would've been caught by now. But in Angel's eyes, Sylvester was the perfect husband and father.

"Honey, you made it just in time to give the sermon," Angel said as soon as Sylvester sat down.

His guilty conscious was starting to get the best of him and he began to think she was suspecting something by the way she was looking at him.

"I'm sorry baby. I was wrapped up in prayer," he lied.

Angel smiled and took her concentration off of the bishop and put it back on the guest pastor. The bishop grabbed some tissue from the stand next to them and wiped his forehead to keep it dry, but it didn't seem to work. He glanced at the congregation to see if Danger sat in the rows directly in front of him and when he didn't see her, he looked back at Angel. He squeezed her hand tight and smiled.

That's what I love about my wife; she's a confident woman and knows her position as my wife will never change. That's something her friends can't understand. People are constantly telling her things, but she doesn't let that faze her at all, he thought while looking her in the eyes. Often times the bishop felt like he didn't deserve Angel, but he wasn't willing to let her go. Plus, they had a beautiful little girl together that they needed to raise.

After church, the bishop, his family, and a handful of deacons and their families all had a huge Thanksgiving dinner together. By the time Sylvester and Angel reached their home, their daughter, Destiny was sound asleep. While Angel tucked their daughter in bed, Sylvester eagerly headed to the office to webcam Danger. He had been thinking about her all day.

"There you are," Danger said as she lay on her bed dressed in the same lingerie that he saw her wear during their first webcam session.

"Why did you come to my church? How did you know it was me?" Sylvester started asking questions as soon as Danger logged on.

"Sssshhhh," she placed her index finger over her lip and instructed the bishop to be quiet. "I'll do all the talking," she said seductively as she came closer to the camera.

The bishop waited in silence. Danger had his full attention.

"Do you enjoy my company? Do you like it when I do this?" she asked while gently massaging her clit.

"Give me a special show," he suggested while his dick began to grow harder and bigger. Any displeasure he'd originally had towards Danger was totally gone.

"Ha-ha. I'm not one of your church members that are at your beck and call." She laughed and pulled her panties up then continued, "Bishop, just as you have expectations, so do I. And I think you know exactly what I want. Because you were disobedient when I saw you earlier, the stakes have gotten higher. Now, instead of five grand, I want seventy-five hundred. If I don't get it, I will ruin your life. Please don't force my hand," Desire stated and quickly logged off the webcam.

"Honey, are you finished with church business yet?" Angel asked while knocking on the door of her husband's home office.

"I'm just about done, pudding," he said before logging off the webcam and shutting down his computer. The bishop's heart was racing and his dick was hard as a rock. Luckily, Angel entered the room ready to play. Her body was perfect as she stood in front of him in her black lingerie. His thoughts immediately went back to Danger.

"Baby, when did you get that?" he asked, trying not to look so guilty.

Angel placed one finger to her lips indicating for Sylvester to keep quiet. He obeyed. Angel was a beast in bed. The bishop had taken much pride in the fact that he had taught her all the tricks she knew. This was one benefit he gained from watching countless pornography videos. He watched as Angel crawled towards him like a frisky tiger. Eager to get inside her, he playfully tackled her. Angel smiled as he positioned himself on top of her. Sylvester caressed Angel's face and started kissing her. He quickly turned her over into a doggie-style position. This was not their usual sex, and Angel was more interested in making love, but Sylvester wanted it rough and hard. He gave Angel long, deep, hard strokes and she screamed out in pain. His mind was completely in another place as he grabbed Angel's hair with one hand and spanked her ass with the other.

"Sylvesterrrrrr," Angel yelled as they came at the same time.

During the entire act, he had Danger, sucking him off, on his mind. Never had he taken money from the church; however, he was now contemplating it. Danger had unleashed something in Sylvester. She was sexy, bold, and mysterious; which was the total opposite of his wife.

"Broken Marriage"

Chapter 2

Isis

"W*wwwhhhhaaaaaaa! Wwwwwhhhaaaaaa!*" Isis was awakened by the screeching yell of her five-month-old son, Jordon.

She rolled over to the left and looked at the clock on her night stand. It read six forty-five a.m. Then she rolled over to the right to see if her husband was sound asleep.

"Hello!" she punched him in the arm.

"What's your problem, Isis?" Vada snapped.

"Don't you hear your damn son crying?" She sat up and got in his face. "He's been crying for five minutes now!"

"So go get him," he said, then rolled over and pulled the covers over his head.

Isis rolled her eyes in disgust, then drug herself out of bed. It was shit like this that made it hard for her to love Vada. It was bad enough they already had a four-year-old daughter and a fucked up relationship. But then she took a charge for him, got married in jail, and then she had the nerve to let his ass get her pregnant again with their son. Isis loved her son, Jordan, and her daughter, Jasmine, but she deeply regretted having them by Vada. Before letting Vada

in her life she was a proud school girl and a God-fearing woman. But she fell for Vada's drug-dealing, fast life. He swept her off her feet sending her into a life of fast money and cars. She was a good girl turned bad. Life was moving so fast that Isis didn't even realize she'd lost herself. It wasn't until she landed in jail that she recognized the mistake she had made. Although Vada vowed to never leave her side and even married her to prove it, Isis blamed him for ruining her life and she could never forgive him. The resentment she held against Vada showed on a daily basis.

Isis slowly lifted her tired body from the bed and headed towards their bedroom door. She stopped at the foot of the bed and glanced over at her sleeping husband. The mere sight of him sleeping so peacefully and snoring like a grizzly bear sent her into a rage. Isis grabbed a handful of the sheets and gripped them tightly, then ripped them off the bed.

"Get the fuck up!" she yelled at the top of her lungs.

Vada jumped up with fire in his eyes. For a moment Isis was afraid, but she refused to let him see the fear in her.

"What you gone do? You jumping up like you gone do something," she said with her hands on her hips.

"Bitch!" Vada threw a pillow at Isis and it smacked her on the side of her face.

Isis quickly picked it up and threw it back at him. He bobbed and weaved like a pro boxer and the pillow flew past him.

"The baby won't stop crying," a small voice interrupted their pillow fight. It was their daughter, Jasmine, and she was carrying her little brother.

"That's a damn shame; Jassie got to get the baby out the

crib because you're too lazy to do it. What kind of mother are you?" Vada said as he got out the bed and began to put his clothes on.

"What kind of father are you? I didn't see your sorry ass budge when the baby was crying either," she said, grabbing Jordon from Jassie's arms, then grabbing Jassie's hand before heading to the kitchen.

She prepared a bottle for her son and cereal for her daughter. As she was feeding Jordon, Vada walked past, heading towards the front door.

"Where do you think you're going?" Isis asked, knowing he didn't usually leave the house so early in the morning.

"To the gym," Vada mumbled as he headed out the door.

As he walked out, it dawned on Isis, *this motherfucker got on jeans.* She wasn't a chick that worked out or even got close to a gym. In fact, Isis swore she was allergic to hard work. In her book, body sculpting consisted of liposuction and botox. But she was smart enough to know you don't wear jeans and Timberland boots to the gym. Her first instinct was to rush to the door and catch Vada before he left, but she knew it would be useless. So Isis called his cell phone instead.

"You have reached the voicemail box of…" the automated message began to play after a few rings and she hung up. Isis immediately pressed redial, and again let the phone ring to voicemail. For the next ten minutes she kept hitting redial and hanging up at the sound of the voicemail.

Eventually Jassie was done with breakfast and it was time to give the kids a bath. Isis got the children bathed and dressed, then she called her girl, Angel. They usually let their daughters get together for a play date every other Saturday. This was also Isis's time to vent about her sorry ass husband.

"Hey Angel," Isis said as soon as her friend answered the phone.

"Hey Isis! What's the plan today?" Angel eagerly asked. She was always so enthusiastic about the girls' play dates. Isis personally would be more excited if she could just drop Jassie off at Angel's house and have some time to herself. Caring for two small children alone was quite draining.

"Well, Jassie has been asking to go to Chuckie Cheese. Are you up for that today?"

"Of course! Let's head there now!"

"Alright. I'll meet you there." Isis hung up the phone.

Isis took her time gathering the kids' things. She had to make sure she packed Jordon's diaper bag with all the necessities for the day. Isis always packed an extra set of clothes, more than enough diapers, extra bottles, a light blanket, a couple small toys, gas medication and Tylenol. Her experinces with her first child taught her the importance of perfectly a packed diaper bag. In addition to Jordan's items, she made sure to pack snacks for Jassie and an extra set of clothes just in case she had an accident.

Once the children were squared away, Isis had to take care of herself. First she drank a glass of Moscato then she packed a mini bottle of Moscato in the diaper bag in case of an emergency. Lastly she turned on Nick Jr. and let the kids watch Sponge Bob while she got dressed. One episode of Sponge Bob and she was ready.

"Okay kids!" she said while placing Jordan in his carrier and grabbing the diaper bag.

They hopped in the car and Isis secured everyone safely in their car seats before driving off. Fifteen minutes later, they were at Chuckie Cheese. She unloaded the children and headed in to the chaotic fun spot for children and dungeon of torture for adults. Isis saw Angel as soon as they walked in.

"Destiny!" Jassie yelled as she ran up to her best friend and hugged her tight.

As the girls chatted away like two little ladies, Angel grabbed Jordon from Isis's hands and hugged her with her free arm. Once they got seated and situated, they let the girls loose to go play and it was time to have some adult conversations. Isis wasted no time telling Angel about her incident earlier in the morning.

"Do you know what Vada's bitch ass did this morning?" she began to say.

"Isis!" Angel stopped her while covering Jordon's tiny ears. "Don't use such language around the baby. I know I can't stop you from cursing, but at least keep those demons away from Jordon."

"Okay Angel," Isis rolled her eyes then continued. "Anyway, so Jordon was crying his butt off and Vada wouldn't even budge to go get him. This dude really feels like he ain't gotta do jack when it comes to these kids! Do you know Jassie got my baby out the crib and brought him to me this morning?"

"Well, wasn't Vada at the studio until late last night?" Angel asked like that was some sort of excuse or something.

"Yeah." Isis said with a blank face.

"Well, maybe he was just tired. You all should work out

some sort of schedule that works for the both of you. You know, as stay-at-home moms, we are expected to do the bulk of caretaking for the children. Raising kids and taking care of home is our job." Angel explained like a proud housewife.

Isis didn't say a word. She just looked at Angel like she was a damn fool. She was trying to figure out just exactly what fucking planet this girl was from. Angel and Isis went way back. She had been her girl since high school, but it was like the older Angel got, the more naive she got. In high school Angel was a strong, independent, black woman and the two of them saw things eye to eye. But ever since she hooked up with the all mighty, Bishop Sylvester Rollins, and was crowned First Lady of Baptist Temple Church, Angel had turned into this holier-than-thou submissive housewife. Isis knew the Lord's Holy Word said something about the man being the head of the household, but damn, there had to be a limit somewhere! Sometimes Isis wondered why she even talked to Angel about her personal marital issues because Angel didn't even recognize her own damn husband's faults.

Everybody in the Christian community knew Bishop Rollins had an addiction to pornography. There were even rumors that he'd had relations with a couple of high-end escorts. But little miss Angel just walked around with a permanent smile like she was oblivious to it all.

"Isis? Are you okay? Did I say something wrong?" Angel asked in response to Isis's silence.

"I'm sorry, Angel. I just have so much on my mind. Let me ask you what you think about this: after the big argument over the baby, Vada gets up and puts on jeans and Timberland boots and heads out the door at seven in the morning. When I asked him where he was headed, he said the gym. Now what man you know wears that attire to the gym?"

"Well, that is kind of strange. Have you talked to him about it?" Angel asked.

"No. I called him several times but it went to voicemail, then he turned his phone off."

"I'm sorry that's not something I can answer. Yes, it does sound strange, but you can't expect the worse because of it. You need to change your way of thinking, Isis. You need to go into the situation feeling confident that there is a reasonable explanation," Angel calmly explained.

Isis felt a slight sense of that same rage that she felt earlier in the morning. Something inside her wanted to just reach out and smack Angel while yelling, "Open your eyes, bitch!" Instead of acting on that anger, she pulled out her emergency bottle of Moscato, poured it into a Chuckie Cheese kid cup, and took a big gulp. She didn't even flinch as she prepared her drink in what seemed like a single motion.

"Isis, please put that away. There are kids and parents all around us. Chuckie himself is even watching," Angel whispered, embarrassed by her friend's obnoxious action.

"They should be more concerned with the children, not me. I ain't hurting nobody by having a drink. Matter of fact, I just may hurt someone if I don't have this drink," Isis said then took another big gulp.

"Skeletons in the Closet"

Chapter 3

Victoria

" **N**ow, Ms. Wade, before you are discharged from the hospital, do you have any questions?" Victoria asked her.

"No, I'm just scared. What if I'm a bad mother to her," the patient said with tears streaming down her face as she held her three-day-old baby in her arms.

"Take a deep breath, three times," Victoria calmly instructed the patient.

"Okay," she nodded her head. Victoria took a small compact mirror out of her medical scrub jacket and placed it in front of the patient's face.

"Do you love your baby? Yes or no?"

"Yes, of course," the patient caressed her daughter's cheek.

"You were destined to have little Abigal Wade. Every day will not be easy. Now say right now, I'm going to be a great mother."

"I'm going to be a great mother," she mumbled.

"Okay that was a good practice run. Now look in the mirror and say it like you mean it!" Victoria held the mirror firm in front of the patient's face.

"I'm going to be a great mother."

"Again."

"I'm going to be a great mother," she said a little louder and more confident.

"Again!"

The patient repeated it two more times; each time a little louder and more confident than the previous time before it. Eventually, a smile, filled with confidence, emerged on her face. Victoria gave her a hug.

"Doctor," the patient said.

"Oh I'm not a doctor. I'm a Physician Assistant. You can call me Victoria."

"Well then, Victoria…thank you." The new mother gave a sincere smile while squeezing Victoria's hand tight.

"You're welcome," Victoria said before leaving the room.

She quickly retreated to her office, closed the door and began to cry to herself. She was hiding a painful secret that her lips couldn't reveal to anyone. She balled up in a fetal position on the love seat that sat in her office and sobbed uncontrollably as her mind drifted back to her dark past.

After a few minutes of gut wrenching crying, Victoria got up from the loveseat and retreated to the window. As she stared out to the street below, she moved her head back and forth in an attempt to relieve some of the tension from her neck. She took a deep breath and closed her eyes. Her heart rate increased, her hands were clammy, and sweat beads formed on her face. She didn't want to go back in the past and relive what happened, but she had this occasional uncontrollable reoccurring need to do so, over and over again, and this was one of those moments.

* * * * *

"Hey Vicky," Bam, the star quarterback of the high school football team said as he approached her.

Bam towered over Victoria, standing at six feet two inches. His broad muscular frame was ideal for sports. He had a perfect smile and dreamy eyes. He was the kind of guy most high school girls dreamed of, but not Victoria.

"Hi," Victoria responded without even looking back. She was the captain of the cheer squad and she was running late for practice.

Bam was known for hitting on all the popular and pretty girls in the school and he usually succeeded in getting any girl he wanted. That alone was enough to turn Victoria off. She prided herself in being a virgin and perfect lady. She was very selective about the guys she dated. She had a squeaky clean reputation and she planned to keep it that way. No way was she going to risk it by dating a scum bag like Bam.

"Hold on. Let me walk with you," Bam insisted.

"Okay, but keep up with me. I've got to get to practice," she stated in an irritated tone as she approached the staircase door of the English hall.

"Well, I won't be long. The party at Dayon's house is coming up on Saturday. I was wondering if you would be interested in going with me," Bam stated.

"No, thanks," she snickered.

"Is something funny?"

"Yes, because everyone knows that I don't date or even deal with high school boys. I prefer college guys. They are more mature and actually have a future," Victoria stated in a condescending tone sure to make Bam feel inferior.

"I'm older than most dudes around here," Bam bragged as he poked out his chest proudly.

"Yeah, that's because you failed seventh grade twice. Remember, we met when you were in that grade the first time," Victoria shook her head and rolled her eyes.

"As long as I graduate, which will be soon, it shouldn't matter how long it took me." Bam said slightly bothered by Victoria's statement.

Bam knew Victoria was the kind of chick that played hard to get. He'd run into many girls like her before. In the beginning they all pretended to be a virgin, or claimed to only date older guys, but if he stayed consistent they always gave in. Bam had tried to get at Victoria plenty of times in the past and she'd always blown him off. He was never really pressed because there were always two girls lined up to take her place. But getting Victoria had become a challenge and Bam was determined to come out the victor.

"Speak for yourself. Thanks for the offer, but I'm not even going to Dayon's party. I have other plans."

"Now, Victoria." Bam cleared his throat. "I asked nicely. I don't take no for an answer." Bam spoke in an assertive tone while staring Victoria dead in the eyes.

"Well, today, October 7th at three in the afternoon will be a first for you. Highlight it, circle it, and save the date on your calendar," she giggled before turning the knob on the staircase door.

Bam pulled out a small knife and grabbed Victoria by the throat. She could feel his hot breath on her cheek. Her heart raced as panic began to set in. She wanted to scream but it was as though she had no voice. She wanted to run but it was as though her feet were frozen in place. So she stood motionless in total shock. "Now, unless you want to get sliced all up in that pretty little face of yours, I suggest you abide by my rules." He whispered in a calm tone as he gently slid the knife across her forehead forcing her hair to the side of her face then kissed her on the cheek. "Not only would it be painful for you if you don't, but you will be left with the scars for the rest of your life. Now lift that skirt up for me," he demanded in an aggressive dominating manner while tugging at the skirt of her cheerleader uniform.

"Okay…okay. Please don't hurt me," Victoria begged as she pretended to lift her skirt.

Once she bent over, she hit Bam in his balls and made a run for it. Unfortunately, Bam was unaffected. The padding from his football pants were designed to protect him from any impact to the groin area. He laughed as he ran after her down the hall and into an empty classroom He cornered her behind a desk near the window. Bam caught a glimpse of the students gathering on the field for after school activities. He knew he didn't have much time before the football coach would realize he wasn't present for practice. "That was a nice try, I'll give you that. Where did you learn that one… some TV show?" Bam forcefully grabbed Victoria by the hair and pressed the knife against her throat. "Now let's try this again," he lifted her skirt as he pushed her against a desk, forcing her to bend over.

Victoria was petrified, but she refused to show any fear. Bam aggressively pushed her chest down on the desk top, and then used his knife to cut off her panties. One slit was all it took. He lifted them to his nose and smelled them before placing them in his book bag as a souvenir. He pulled out his penis and attempted to shove it in her.

"Ah shit! This some tight pussy!" Bam said realizing he hadn't penetrated her at all.

"Don't tell me I'm about to dig into some virgin pussy 'cause that might make me cum sooner than I want to." Bam spat on his erect penis hoping it would add lubrication.

He smiled at the thought of getting some virgin pussy. Once his dick was soaked in saliva, he grabbed Victoria by the waist and thrust his hips forward forcing himself deep inside her. He moaned with pure satisfaction when he heard a popping sound.

"Aaaahhhhhh!!!!!!" Victoria screamed out in pain.

"Hell yeah! You little fucking slut. You like this dick don't you? Say yes over and over and over again. Tell me how you love this dick," Bam demanded.

"Noooooo," Victoria screamed, but no one could hear her. Her screams were no competition with the chaotic sounds of the band playing, the football team practicing and the cheering squad cheering. Her body trembled with pain. Every muscle was tightened and she struggled to breathe as she fought through the moments of agony that seemed to last forever.

"I said, say yes," Bam demanded as he pressed the end of his knife into the side of her neck.

"Yes," she whispered as tears streamed down her face.

"Louder, you little slut," he demanded.

"Yes, yes, yes," Victoria uttered between tears.

"More…don't stop saying it. I'm about to cum in this

tight pussy!"

"Yes, yes, yes, yes." Victoria forced out the words hoping it would put an end to the torture. Although Bam had a knife to her neck it felt as though he was ripping her insides apart.

"Aaah," he moaned while exploding inside Victoria.

"Man, you got some good pussy," he said while panting. His tone came across more as a satisfied lover describing the nutt of his life instead of a rapist. "Clean that shit up," he smacked Victoria on the ass and then pointed to the semen mixed with blood that ran down the inside of her thigh. "I guess I better head to practice now and you need to get to that cheerleading thing you do. Thanks for the nutt slut," he said while pulling up his pants, "...it was just what I need to get through the day." Bam walked out the room, never looked back.

Victoria laid on the desk for several minutes sobbing and breathing heavily in total shock. Once she gathered herself, she ran out of the classroom and straight into a cleaning cart in the hallway.

"Miss, are you all right?" the janitor asked while sweeping and noticing her stumble on his cart.

Victoria didn't respond, she just ran out of the school as fast as she could. She hopped in her car and drove home. The door slammed behind her as she ran up the stairs and took the hottest shower she could stand. As the scolding water ran down her body she scrubbed harder and harder making her flesh welt as she tried to get Bam's scent off of her skin. She didn't even come down for dinner that day. Her bed and her pillow were her only source of comfort as she cried herself to sleep.

As the weeks passed, Victoria experienced a number of changes. Her vagina seemed to be in constant pain, with a heavy discharge. Eventually a foul odor developed. It became so bad that others began to smell it. Each day, sometimes twice a day, Victoria was bathed using feminine wash and powdered her crotch with feminine power. She would drown her body in Victoria Secret body spray and lotion in hopes of masking the smell. That worked initially, but within a matter of hours it always wore off.

One day while in the locker room, she noticed some the girls from the cheerleading squad whispering and looking in her direction. Then when she walked closer to them, they instantly ceased all conversation. Deep inside she knew they were talking about her. Nevertheless, she headed to her locker as though she wasn't even fazed by their childish chatter. While at her locker, one of her fellow cheer mates took her aside. She told her exactly what the girls were saying about her. At that moment Victoria showed no emotion, but after school she cried to herself on the way home. When she met up with her best friend, Desire, she told her what had been said. Desire had been her friend since elementary school, but Desire's parents couldn't afford private school like Victoria's so she went to a local public school nearby. They met each day after school to hang out. Victoria knew Desire would know exactly what to do. Without hesitation she reassured her friend, then offered to go with her to the health department.

"It's probably gonorrhea," Desire said with no shame. "I've had it twice. They simply treat it with antibiotics."

DESIRE

Victoria didn't respond, she just put her head down and walked away totally embarrassed and ashamed. She didn't even bother defending herself. It was a missed opportunity for Victoria to tell her bestie what had happened to her—how she'd been raped by the star football player—but instead, she remained silent; burying her secret deep within.

"Oh, I'm sorry best friend. I forgot, you're a virgin," Desire said sarcastically.

She never did believe Victoria when she would tell her she had never had sex. Desire figured Victoria was just trying to preserve her good-girl image. Desire, on the other hand, was promiscuous and showed no shame about it. She had all the latest fashions and jewelry and all the guys wanted a piece of her. She was known as *Mac and Cheese* to guys around the neighborhood. They called her that because her pussy was so wet it sounded like someone stirring macaroni and cheese. Victoria could never understand why Desire, such a pretty girl with such a great family, would act that way. After all, Victoria did all she could to make the honor roll, speak proper English, and conduct herself as a lady at all times.

For the first time, Victoria was no longer the perfect, popular high school girl everyone envied. In a matter of one month, her entire world had begun to crumble. Determined to protect her squeaky-clean reputation, Victoria snuck off to a local health clinic. The doctor informed her she had pelvic inflammatory disease and prescribed an antibiotic to clear up the infection. He explained to her the effects of PID would lead to infertility and/or complications with giving birth due to the excessive scar tissue. He wanted her to take her medication and follow up with a few to tests to ensure the infection was gone and to examine the effects of the disease. Victoria took the medication as ordered, but did not follow up as directed. A part of her didn't want to know the effects of her STD. All she wanted was to put that whole experience behind her and move forward. Victoria was only sixteen and she was crumbling under the expectations of her parents. All they wanted to see was stellar grades and have the illusion of a picture-perfect Christian family; and by no means was Victoria going to let them down.

After graduating high school, Victoria said goodbye to her best friend, her high school and the horrible secret attached to it. She attended the prestigious Duke University, graduated with a Masters of Health Science with honors and passed her Physician Assistant National Certifying Exam on the first try. With her father being on the committee board for the city of Charlotte, North Carolina, and having some friends who had influence at Carolinas Medical Center, Victoria was handed a lucrative position as a Physician Assistant on the Labor and Delivery unit as a new graduate.

* * * * *

On the outside, Victoria had a picture perfect life; a lavish home, truck, car and miniature Yorkie named Chanel. The only thing that was missing was a husband and a child. She longed for a husband, but never let any man get too close in fear of getting hurt. Also, Victoria figured what man would want her knowing she possibly couldn't conceive a child? Deep inside, Victoria felt she wasn't worthy of a good man.

The ranting of the word "little slut" constantly resurfaced in her mind. She could never forget those words Bam used repeatedly while she was being raped.

Victoria was approaching her thirties, and her mother had begun getting the grandma itch; but first, Victoria needed to get married. It had come to the point where Victoria made it a habit to avoid her mother's calls. She felt she could never satisfy her mother; in fact she was tired of trying. She was trying to portray perfection and tired of living for her parents. No one had a clue how truly miserable she was.

Knock, Knock! There was an unexpected knock on her office door.

"Yes, coming," she jumped up, wiped her tears away with her fingers and opened the door.

"Room ten, her water just broke," the nurse announced.

"I'll be right there!"

"A Stranger in My House"

Diamond Diva
SERIES

Chapter 4

Angel

Bannnnnnngggggg! Angel woke up to a loud sound in the midst of the darkness. The only thing she could see were the red numbers on the alarm clock that read, 5:00 a.m. She was scared out her mind. Her first thought was her baby girl, Destiny, and making sure she was safe. Her second thought was her loving husband, Sylvester, and wondering if he had heard the same noise that woke her. Angel didn't see Sylvester in bed next to her, so she reached over to his side of the bed. Her hands slid across their satin sheets and she quickly realized her husband was not in bed. All sorts of thoughts ran through her mind, *Is Sylvester ok? What if he has fallen? What if someone has attacked him?* Angel sat frozen in fear. She didn't even think to hit the alarm button on the panel that was on the wall near her bedroom door. As she sat motionless, she heard another sound. But this sound was quite familiar. It was the sound of someone slowly creeping up the stairs. Scared to tears, Angel wanted to scream the name of Jesus and demand protection from the heavens above. Instead she chose to drop to her knees clasp her hands together and pray.

"Our Father who art in heaven, Hallowed be thy name; Thy Kingdom come," Angel whispered the Lord's Prayer as the sound of the footsteps got closer and closer and the last step creaked.

"Baby what are you praying about so feverishly this early in the morning?" Sylvester asked while standing over his wife.

Angel slowly lifted her head and thanked God before answering him.

"Really, honey?" Angel said with a bit of sarcasm as she stood to her feet. "You come in here at five in the morning scaring me half to death, and then have the nerve to ask me what I'm praying about."

"Calm down baby, I know I probably scared you, but it wasn't intentional," Sylvester said as he hurried into the bathroom and started to undress himself.

Angel watched quietly as he took off his clothes. She noticed he didn't have to unhook his belt, unbutton his pants or unzip them, but she didn't say a word. As a woman that didn't jump to conclusions, she remained calm and patiently waited for an explanation. But instead of changing into his pajamas, brushing his teeth and coming to bed as Angel expected, Sylvester turned on the water and hopped in the shower. Ten minutes later he came out the bathroom with his pajamas on.

"I know that look," he said as he curled up in bed beside his wife and playfully kissed her all over her face.

Angel smiled and any bit of anger she felt had totally disappeared. "Baby, are you going to tell me why you're just now coming to bed this time of morning?" she asked, searching for answers.

"I was downstairs in my office working on some things and I fell asleep. I was surprised when I woke up and saw the time. I thought for sure you would have come and waken me," Sylvester explained, then laid back and pulled the covers over his head and went to sleep.

Angel still didn't have an answer for the unbuttoned pants, but she didn't bother mentioning it. She really wanted to believe her husband, but it was just something about this situation that created a terrible feeling in the bottom of her stomach. Angel was a true believer that what goes on in the dark would soon come to light, so she just let it go and went back to sleep.

Nearly an hour later, she was greeted by her beautiful daughter. Destiny was already awake, before the alarm clock sounded. Angel had to wonder if her sleep was broken by her parents little incident earlier that morning.

"Good morning Mommy and Daddy!" Destiny said with excitement.

Sylvester lifted his head slightly off his pillow and mumbled, "Hi baby," then he dropped his head again.

Angel gave her daughter a big smile and replied, "Mommy's up honey. Now let's get this pretty little girl ready for school."

The way Sylvester came to bed earlier that morning was still fresh on Angel's mind, but she had to pull it all together for her daughter's sake. She never wanted Destiny to see her mommy and daddy fight or even to have the slightest idea there was a problem between them. As Destiny rushed off to her room to get ready for school, Angel headed to the bathroom to take a shower. When she walked in she noticed Sylvester's clothes from the night before were still lying in the middle of the bathroom floor. The curious side of Angel wanted to search his pockets for any signs of infidelity, but the confident wife inside of her soon took over. Instead of searching his pockets like an insecure woman, Angel simply picked his clothes up and placed them in the wicker laundry basket that sat in the bathroom corner. Then she turned on the shower and forced herself inside. As the hot water ran down her back and down the drain she prayed it took all her negative thoughts with it. After getting dressed, she went downstairs and cooked an amazing breakfast for Destiny and Sylvester.

Then with a big smile she walked back to the bedroom where her husband slept, gently placed her hand on his shoulder and whispered in his ear, "Breakfast is ready whenever you feel like eating, honey."

"Thank you baby, it smells good." He replied, still half asleep.

"Have a great day honey!" She responded as she walked away.

As far as Sylvester knew everything was fine; but deep down inside, Angel still had some unanswered questions. So after dropping Destiny off at school and running a few errands, she decided to pay her older brother a visit and get some much needed advice. She could hear Isis voice in her head, *Honey when it comes to finding out the truth about a man, one has to ask another man.* Angel would never confide to any other male other than her brother or father. Her brother had been assisting with some renovations at the church during the week, so she knew exactly where to find him. She arrived at the church around lunch time with his favorite meal. He loved meatloaf served with a huge piece of Jiffy cornbread and candied yams. As soon as he saw her walk in, he immediately received her with open arms and a gigantic smile.

"Hey sissy!" he called her by the nickname he had used for her since they were kids. Angel would always be *little sister* in his eyes. Her brother wasn't always the prefect child, but he always encouraged her to do what was right. And this was definitely a time that she needed guidance from her big brother.

"Hey big brother!" she said with a smile, trying to hide the pain she felt inside.

"What's wrong sissy?" he asked, seeing right through her poor disguise. He watched her eyes closely. The twinkle and glow she normally had was now dark and dim. "You didn't come all the way up here just to give me my favorite meal." He threw his arm across her shoulder. He had a way of making her feel like a little school girl. She could never keep anything from him even if she tried.

"Something is going on in my marriage and I need some manly advice right now," Angel said as she held her head down in shame.

"You know what pop used to always say, 'No matter what it is, God can work it out'," he responded.

That was their father's response to everything and that's the same way he raised his family to believe. They had listened to him say that a million times before, and Angel actually believed it, but this time was different. She felt God had placed her in a situation where her faith was being tested. Before her little situation earlier that morning, Angel thought that she had the perfect marriage. At this point, she didn't know what to believe anymore. All of sudden, she broke down and started crying on her brother's shoulder.

"Whyyyyy would he do this to me?" she said between sobs.

Her brother took her in his arms and hugged her tightly. He didn't say a word as he watched her let out all the emotions she had bottled inside. Her face rested on his shoulders as her tears wet his tee-shirt. Angel never got the strength to tell him what happened, but it seemed like he already knew the whole story. Her brother rocked her back and forth assuring her that everything was going to be alright. After a couple of minutes of crying, she managed to finally get herself together. She just sat in silence staring at her brother. She was waiting for him to say something and for a reaction from him to her pain. After a few moments, he finally spoke.

"Even if he doesn't know how to love you right, there is always one man that will never let you down."

Understanding his answer, but still not feeling complete, Angel hugged him and walked away. She needed to hear more. This was one time the Word alone wasn't good enough. She knew all about the Bible and could read scriptures for days. This time Angel wanted some raw, straight-up advice and she knew exactly who to get it from. Once she got home she called her longtime friend, Isis.

"Hello," she answered on the first ring.

"Hey," Angel sighed.

"Oh, lawd! I know that sound. What the hell is wrong, girl?"

"What do you mean?" Angel asked, still deciding if she

really wanted to tell Isis what was truly going on.

Angel hated getting anyone involved in her marriage, especially since she was the First Lady and her husband was the great Bishop Sylvester Rollins of the Baptist Temple Church. The last thing she needed was her family's great name caught up in the middle of a scandal. Angel didn't like for anyone to judge Sylvester. She wanted people of the community to look up to him, not down at him. Besides, she felt as though she would be committing an act of sin by gossiping.

"Come on Angel. We both know you didn't call me for nothing. There is something on your mind, so let's hear it!" Isis demanded.

"Well," Angel took a deep breath then continued, "I woke up at five in the morning and Sylvester wasn't in the bed," she said quickly then exhaled.

"Okay, so where was he?" Isis impatiently asked before Angel could get another word in.

"He claimed that he was in his office"

"Doing what? Oh, let me guess…he was praying for his church members. Oh, better yet…he was getting prepared for next week's sermon, right?" Isis said full of sarcasm.

"No, he simply said that he was working on some things and fell asleep."

"Okay, let me keep it one hundred and ten with you. I don't believe it and neither should you." Isis said firmly.

It was no secret that Sylvester was addicted to porn. That rumor had been stirring around the church for at least six months. Angel was the only one who didn't know. At this particular time, Isis didn't have the heart to tell her. She wanted to be there for her friend, but she also wanted Angel to smarten up and stop being so naive.

"Well, him coming to bed at 5:00 a.m. isn't the worse part of the story," Angel paused then continued, "When he finally came upstairs, his pants were unbuttoned and as soon as he entered the bedroom, he immediately headed to the bathroom and showered." Angel's stomach turned as she told the story.

"You're not going to want to do this; however, you're going to have to start being a detective," Isis stated.

Angel didn't respond. She just sat on the phone in silence.

"Hello??? Are you on board or not?"

"I guess," Angel said hesitantly. She knew her friend was about to take her into unwarranted territory.

"Okay. Go into his office. I'm gonna stay on the phone with you for moral support. I would just give you instructions, but I know if I did, you would never go through with it alone."

"Alright," Angel reluctantly agreed before she tiptoed downstairs.

She didn't like feeling like a snooper. Angel was never the jealous type. She figured acting that way would drive her crazy. Besides as the saying goes, "If you look, you shall find." And honestly she felt denial was much safer.

"Okay, I'm here," Angel said after reaching Sylvester's office.

"Okay, now sit at his desk," Isis gave her next instruction.

"Okay. Now what?"

"Just look at his surroundings. Does anything look strange?"

Angel laid back in her husband's office chair and looked around the office. There was nothing that immediately jumped out at her at first glance.

"This is ridiculous. I'm going back upstairs," Angel said as she stood up and headed towards the door.

She stopped at the table in the corner to turn off his lamp and that's when she noticed something.

"Our family picture," she said to Isis.

"What about it?" she asked.

"It's lying flat on the table."

"Okay, now go back to his desk and sit in the chair." Isis paused long enough for Angel to do so then continued. "When you look over your shoulder do you see the picture behind you?"

"Yes. It's over my left shoulder," Angel said wondering what Isis was getting at.

"Turn on his laptop." Isis knew exactly what was about to be revealed, but she was glad it happened this way instead of having to tell her best friend herself.

"Okay."

"Now search his history and tell me what you see." Isis waited patiently.

Angel was in shock as she scrolled through his history. It was full of porn sites, one after another. Her stomach turned in disgust as she glanced at them.

"So, what do you see?" Isis asked.

"Well...he's looking at pornographic websites," Angel said with disappointment. "But this doesn't explain his unbuttoned pants, the hurried shower or why the family picture is turned down."

"Dig deeper, Angel. If his boxers from last night aren't washed already, take a glimpse at his boxers and see if he has white cum stains in them. Plus, if the boxers are dark, that's a sure giveaway. If you witnessed these two vital hints, Sylvester has cheated on you."

This time, Angel ran upstairs only touching every other step. She ran into the bedroom, and rummaged through the dirty clothes basket. Sylvester's boxers were dark and there were cum stains all over them. Angel froze in place, leaned against the bathroom wall and slid to the floor. Isis could hear Angel sobbing uncontrollably.

"I'm so sorry, Angel. I know it hurts. You have two choices: either stay and work it out, or leave. I will support you either way. No woman wants to break up their happy home, especially when a child is involved," Isis tried to be supportive.

"I don't know, Isis. I feel numb. I can't believe this is happening to me," Angel said while cradling herself in the corner of the bathroom.

"I can't believe it either," Isis lied.

"Maybe, it's not what we think. Maybe this cum stain is from him jerking off while looking at the porn sites. I can't wrap my brain around my husband even being capable of the ultimate betrayal of cheating."

"Scheming Sunday"

Diamond Diva
SERIES

Chapter 5

Desire

Desire was still continuing her business with her online videos and private shows. At this point, she was charging double to her regular customers. Her number one customer had somehow slipped passed her rate increase. Not only had the bishop not logged on in days, but he had not owned up to his financial obligation either. Desire didn't like being ignored mixed with the debt of money. It was time for the bishop to pay...with interest. Desire had sucked his dick and now he was acting like she didn't exist anymore, or simply as if he wanted her to go away. It irritated Desire that the bishop portrayed this perfect leader image in public that people envied; however, in the wee hours of the morning, he was a sex-crazed man.

Too many days had passed, and Desire hadn't heard from the bishop so she figured it was time she paid him a little visit. So once again she put on her Sunday best and headed to Baptist Temple Church. The parking lot was full as she parked her car and headed in. This time she was a little late, so she decided to sit in the congregation and wait to see the bishop after service. She saw a spot in a pew not

too far from the front and headed in that direction to sit down.

"Good morning…Praise the Lord!" she said as she walked past several church members. Desire was good at putting on a front.

Once she found her seat she sat down and placed her Bible on her lap. This day she played the role of the perfect Christian woman well. Desire didn't stand because she didn't want to bring too much attention to herself. After all, she was there on a stalker mission. All she wanted to do was slither in and slither away to get the bishop's attention. After the fourth church song and five church members fell slain in the Spirit, the bishop and his wife, Angel—with their daughter, walked out into the congregation. Not a speck of makeup was on Angel's face. She had natural beauty. She looked sharp—as the First Lady—in her navy blue suit that didn't reveal a bit of cleavage. A man approached Desire; distracting her agenda for the moment.

"Excuse me, Miss, is anyone sitting here?" he whispered because the choir was singing during praise and worship and he didn't want to interrupt anyone.

"No," she said shaking her head.

This man looked to be a little over six feet tall. Desire always made it a practice to take notice of tall, dark and handsome men. He had curly hair and she could see a tattoo on his neck that was mainly shielded by the collar of his shirt. She noticed a nice smile and Spice Bomb cologne lingering in the air. He was a little on the slim side, but Desire didn't mind. She couldn't help but admire him the entire service. She made it her business to give him the eye to let him know she was interested. She could tell by his subtle smile and wink of an eye that he picked up on her flirtatious vibe. After the sermon, the bishop gave the benediction.

"I apologize for arriving to church late and disrupting you with my tardiness. The devil was busy and doing all he could this morning to hinder me from attending church," the man explained.

"It's all right. In the end you prevailed. At least, you arrived here safe and sound," Desire said.

"Most people give you the evil eye when arriving late. Hi, I'm Bam by the way," he said, extending his hand for a shake.

"Hi, I'm Desire," she replied shaking his hand.

"It's a pleasure to meet you. I don't usually mingle with the church crowd. I have to admit, I come here to get the Word and go. Here's my number, call me when you have a moment," Bam said pulling a card out of his pocket.

"Maybe, I will," she nodded her head while taking the card.

When glancing at the card, she noticed Mr. Bam was a private contractor. It looked as though he owned his own contracting company. Desire watched as Bam walked to the exit doors with other church members and she also noticed that she had caught the bishop's eye when he was speaking with another church member. As she walked closer to the bishop, his facial expression immediately changed. He turned white as a ghost. It was almost as if he was going to pass out on the spot. Meanwhile, a rush of adrenaline penetrated through Desire's body. It infuriated her to be ignored, taken advantage of, and looked at as a mere joke.

Worst of all, she didn't get her money and she despised men who beat around the bush. During their last conversation, Desire was convinced the bishop had no intentions of fulfilling his financial obligation to her.

Out of the right corner of her eye, Desire caught a glimpse of the bishop's wife and daughter approaching him. Sylvester rushed to pick up his daughter. Quickly, Desire acted as if she had misplaced something on the church pew where she sat.

"Me and Destiny are gonna head home. What would you like for dinner, honey?" Desire heard his wife ask.

She felt pity for his wife. Angel was living a delusion of a so-called life. There she was thinking her husband is a wonderful church leader comparable to Moses, and just a great husband. Yet he was soliciting cybersex and tricking with Desire. Desire never wanted to be in a situation like Angel, where another woman had one up on her.

Within a few minutes, the bishop walked away from his wife and daughter to speak with more members of the church. Suddenly, Bam entered back into the sanctuary and headed to the bishop's wife and daughter. Hugs were exchanged and a bit of small talk. Desire wondered what connection these people had to each other. More importantly, she wondered if she could use Bam to her advantage to gather information from him that could help her get the money she sought after.

Bam eventually wondered off toward the back of the church and Desire diverted her attention back to the bishop's wife and daughter. She noticed his daughter dancing on her tippy toes with a worried look on her face. Desire knew that look well because she was guilty of it herself as a child. The little girl had to use the bathroom. Moments later, the wife and daughter quickly walked to the restroom.

Bishop finished up his conversation with the small group of people he was speaking with and headed to his office. Desire knew it was the perfect time to strike. She followed closely behind him. She hoped to be walking out of the church with cash in hand or at least a confirmation for a wire transfer.

Desire walked in the bishop's office and slowly closed the door behind her. He shrugged his shoulders in disgust then asked, "What are you doing here, again? I told you that I don't have the money."

"Please, you're a prick. Don't you dare give me *that* face," she said.

"I just want some peace in my life. You could destroy my family with your lies. The sex was consensual—what you need to understand is that it was also free. I don't pay for sex, sexual favors, or any other indiscretions I might have had in the past. Look, I'm a Bishop. I need to act like one. What I did was wrong. I apologize. Now please see yourself out of my office and out of my church," Sylvester demanded.

"I'm not going anywhere. You *do* pay for sex, especially cybersex. You were my highest paying customer. I even came here to pay you a friendly visit and now you don't want to pay—after services have been rendered?"

"You willingly came down to the church and seduced me."

"Bishop, you certainly didn't stop me."

"Lady, you think you're the only woman that I have

had extracurricular activities with over the years?" he asked chuckling.

"Cool that tone of yours. Now you're going to give me ten thousand in cash or through a wire transfer; your choice. I still haven't received my money. I was able to get a copy of all the email addresses of your church members the last time I was in your office. A word of advice, put a password on your computer. You have a week to get me my money; this time, there won't be any more warnings. Listen, I know your background. You come from a long line of pastors and bishops and you've never really had a real job. After this leaks, you'll be living an entirely different life... a divorce, only weekend visits with that beautiful daughter of yours, and that grand house of yours will be going to your wife. The ball's in your court Bishop, you make the choice," Desire explained.

"But..."

"Bishop, I don't care what you have to say. Get me the money," she said after cutting him off and handing him a deposit slip.

"You're harassing me and my family. I could have you arrested."

"You're worried about harassment when your entire church career is on the line. Wow, you really are stupid. I have ten thousand dollars dancing in my mind, already," Desire giggled before walking out of the office.

When she closed the door, other church members were still in the sanctuary chatting away. She straightened her dress and put back on her perfect Christian persona. As she was leaving, she noticed Bam came from the other side of the church and entered the bishop's office. She hoped he hadn't seen her come out of the office.

"Married to a Rapper"

Chapter 6

Isis

"Yooooo!!!!!!" Vada sang into the phone as soon as Isis picked up.

"What you so excited about?" Isis asked as she picked their son up and propped him on her hip.

"Guess who just got signed to Hungry Pups Record Label?" he said full of joy before screaming, "Vance Davon Harris!" He screamed his government name into the phone.

For the first time in years, he wasn't afraid to say his real name. He didn't give a shit who was listening in on this particular phone call. A nigga was finally doing a legit hustle!

Hungry Pups was one of the leading recording labels at the time. They had signed all of the hottest artists topping the charts. The average chick would have been celebrating at the sound of that news, but not Isis. Instead, her brain instantly shifted to the numerous groupies, bitches, hood rats, and two-dollar whores that would be after her man.

"Oh. That's good...I guess," Isis mumbled.

"Damn, you don't sound like you proud of a nigga," Vada said, noticing the lack of enthusiasm in her voice.

"I mean, you knew this day would come, right? So what's

the big deal?"

"You really are a miserable chick. Nothing makes you happy. Well, if nothing else, be glad a nigga can take care of his home without selling drugs and getting locked up."

"You mean without getting his girl locked up," Isis said, reminding him that she was the one that went to jail for his drugs, and not him.

As much as Isis wanted to, she could never forgive Vada for sending her to jail and taking her away from her daughter. She missed an entire year of her daughter's life. A few months after she was released from jail, she had another child. It seemed as though her entire life had be taken from her in a short amount of time. She started dating Vada at a young age and got pregnant during high school. She had Jassie right after graduation; so instead of going to nursing school after high school like she'd planned, she ended up not attending college at all. Then she got wrapped up in the fast life of drugs, and money; so college was a non-factor at that point. It wasn't until she got locked up that reality hit. Although she was in jail for only a short stay, it was long enough to make her realize she'd made some really bad mistakes. While in jail, she sought God, prayed daily and vowed to come out a new person. With the help of her old cell mate, Desire, she was planning to get out and live in the lap of luxury, but from legit resources. No more hood rich shit. But just like everyone else, that was all just jail talk—shit you say while locked up. When Isis hit the streets, it was back to what she left…a drug-dealing boyfriend, no education, and a whole lot of bullshit. She'd lost contact with Desire, and no one else would encourage her, or believe in her, like

Desire did.

"Aight Isis. Well, tonight Jay V is having a show at Cameo and they gonna introduce me as the newest artist added to the label. I got a little advance money and shit, so I was thinking we can go get fresh for this shit and go as a couple," Vada said sincerely.

"Nah, you can have that. I'm good."

"I already rented a car and got us a nice ass room uptown and everything, Isis," Vada said sounding almost like he was begging.

"I said, I'll pass!" Isis said before hanging up the phone.

Vada didn't even bother calling her back. There was no way he was gonna let Isis's miserable ass ruin his night. He looked at the time and it was almost six in the evening, so he only had a short amount of time to get ready for the night. He rushed to South Park Mall. He started with Neiman Marcus to get a fresh outfit, then he hit up Louis Vuitton for a pair of sneakers and a belt. After that, he was off to the barbershop to get a fresh cut.

"Sup, niggas!" Vada announced after coming through the front door of the barbershop with his hands up in the air.

"Where have you been hiding?" Nino asked while finishing a customer's haircut.

For the last five years, Nino had been Vada's barber. There were times when Vada was broke as hell and couldn't even pay for a cut; Nino would do it anyway. Nino always saw potential in Vada and encouraged him to get off the block. He would say, "There's no name on the block for you, Vada."

"Give me a minute, I'll be right with you," Nino said,

G Street Chronicles / 69

wondering why the hell everyone at the shop, except for him, was staring out the window. He walked to the window and saw a Black Porsche Panamera parked outside.

"What's up with the new whip?" a dude asked.

He was a guy from Vada's old neighborhood where he grew up. It made Vada's dick hard seeing these niggas at the window gawking over his car while wishing they were him. The best part was, they had no clue the vehicle was rented. He thrived on being number one.

Four years ago, the whole neighborhood's drug operation belonged to him. But one day, Vada had gotten a little too comfortable and that's when the narcotics agents decided to strike. The crazy thing is, Vada had a sick sense something was about to go down weeks before it actually happened. He'd noticed one of his soldiers that went by the name Glock had begun to move strange. At times he would be gone for days with no excuse. Glock wouldn't answer his phone and he had begun to act real shady. Vada knew this was out of character for him but he wasn't sure if the guy was getting high, had a little silent beef with him or was working with the police. If Vada had used his better judgment, he would have cut Glock off right away. Instead, he let greed take over. Clouded by the vision of dollar signs dancing in his heads, he ignored his soldier's strange behavior and continued business as usual. Vada and Isis headed to meet Glock to give him a drop like they did every week. This time as soon as they handed it over, narcotics agents came from everywhere, flooding the scene. Vada later found out Glock had gotten a dope charge and copped a plea to work. He agreed to work as a confidential informant for a lighter sentence.

Isis had taken the wrap for Vada. Otherwise, He would have gone away to God knows where, ruining all of his dreams of ever becoming a rapper. Deep inside he felt less of a man for letting his baby mama take the wrap for him. He vowed to make it up to her. He knew she resented him for that, and he wished that she wouldn't hate him for the rest of their lives. Even though Vada didn't say it much, he really did love his wife.

"I just got signed to a record label," Vada said.

"You're next," Nino said, inviting Vada to his chair.

"Congrats on that record deal, homie. I'm proud of you," his homeboy said, then gave him a dap.

"Thanks, Nino. Here's a little something to show my appreciation for hooking me up all these years," Vada replied, handing him five hundred dollars.

"Nah, duke. You ain't gotta do that," Nino pushed the money away.

"Come on, man. You have always looked out for me. I'll never forget where I came from and the people who have helped me," he said, sliding the wad of money in Nino's barber jacket.

"So listen, come through to Cameo's tonight to the Jay V show. I'm having my official crowning to the squad and doing a little performance." Vada handed Nino a VIP wrist band.

After talking about old memories for over an hour, it was time for Vada to head out. By the time Vada left the barber shop, it was nearly ten o'clock. Time was really creeping up on him, so instead of heading home, he went straight to the hotel room to get dressed. He figured he would leave for the club straight from there.

"What's up Vada," a female voice said as he headed to the hotel elevator.

He looked back to see one of Isis's hood rat friends. She was giving him the side eye like she knew he was up to no good. He started to call her out on it, but figured it wasn't worth it. This was the best day of his life besides the birth of his kids, and he refused to let Isis or her hood friends ruin it.

"What's up, yo?" he said then hopped on the elevator. He wanted no conversation with this chick. He could tell by the look in her eyes that she was bad news.

As soon as Vada reached his room, he jumped in the shower. By the time he got out, he had three missed calls from Isis. Although he didn't want her to kill his vibe, he still returned her call. She was his wife and the mother of his kids, so he had to make sure everything was okay.

"How many times do I have to call in order for you to answer?" Isis yelled.

"I was in the shower," Vada calmly responded while pulling his clothes out the bag and popping the tags.

"Shower? Where are you?"

"The hotel," he said, knowing the hood chick from earlier had already told Isis he was there and that was why she was blowing him up.

"Oh, really? You already fucking bitches, huh?"

"Nope. Not at all. I'm in room 205; you can come by if you want," Vada said nonchalantly.

"Like I said earlier, I'll pass," Isis snapped.

"Well, aight. I'm about to get dressed, so I'll hit you later," Vada said, then hung up the phone.

He was right, Isis was calling because her homegirl had just hit her up saying she saw him at the hotel. Then when Isis called him and he didn't answer she just knew for sure he was with a chick. She was convinced this new *rap artist lifestyle* was gonna be the end of their relationship. For a minute, she actually thought about getting dressed and popping up at the club, but after trying on a few dresses, and looking like a stuffed turkey, she decided not to go. After the birth of her son, Isis never bounced back to her perfect hourglass shape. She had a permanent pudge and her booty no longer sat up like a ripe tomato. Frankly, she hated the woman she saw when she looked in the mirror.

Ringggggg, the sound her of house phone interrupted her pity party. She looked at the caller ID and it read Sylvester Rollins. It was Angel calling from her house phone. At first thought Isis didn't want to speak to Angel, but right before the last ring she answered.

"Hello?"

"Hey girl," Angel greeted her.

"Hi."

"Whatcha doing?"

"Oh, just wondering why I married Vada and why I feel so damn fat. After baby boy was born, I finally have realized that I will never get my hour glass shape back. Plus, Vada got a brand new record deal and I know the bitches and entourage are coming. This time next year, I may be filing for divorce. It's irritating the chaos that comes with a record deal." Isis went on ranting tantrum.

"A new record deal? That's exciting news. Pray and have faith that Vada won't stray and will make wise choices on the road," Angel advised.

"Angel, you're always so optimistic. I need some of that. Anyway, enough about me. What is going on with you, your daughter, and hubby?" Isis changed the subject.

"My little one is fine, getting taller and looking like her father each day that passes. As far as Sylvester, I still haven't spoken to him about what I discovered. I mean, he wasn't actually cheating. So there's no reason to make a big deal out of it."

"Angel, cybersex is cheating. You need to address that with him sooner than later."

"But, I have no hard evidence."

"Well, maybe, you're right. I have my own issues at this very moment, and I definitely don't want to be putting ideas in your head. I will advise you to be mindful and maybe do a bit more detective work," Isis suggested.

"I will. I just don't want to be so negative. Sylvester needs support...our whole family does. Pray for me."

"Of course I will. Let me get off the phone so I can clean up the kitchen," Isis said.

"Okay. I will call you later on this week," Angel agreed.

"Okay."

After speaking to Angel, Isis figured maybe she was being a bit negative. She decided to have a different attitude and be more supportive of her husband. After feeding the kids and giving them a bath, she put them to bed and gave Vada a call. She wanted to apologize for her actions earlier in the day, tell him congrats, and wish him good luck on his performance.

Ring, ring, ring....Vada noticed his phone ringing. It was

Isis but instead of answering, he decided to let the phone go to voicemail. He took the last pull off his blunt as he sat in his car in front of the club, blasting his music. Deep down, Vada was a bit nervous and a little weed was all he needed to get right.

Minutes later Vada hopped out his whip and headed in the club. After the doors opened, a rush of adrenaline pulsated through his body. So many people had come through to show him love. This was his night! He rushed to the VIP section amped up.

"Yo! Where the bartender at?" he asked as soon as he walked up.

"We got you!" his boys from the record label said, noticing he had finally arrived.

Buzz, buzz, buzz....Vada noticed his phone vibrating in his pocket. He looked at it and it was Isis calling again. And like before, he decided to let the phone go to voicemail. He was in the club now and it was way too noisy; he figured he wouldn't be able to hear her anyway if he answered. Sure he could have gone to the bathroom to speak to her, but honestly, he wasn't interested in hearing the negative shit she always had to say. Secretly, Vada wished Isis was there to share in his success because if it wasn't for her, he wouldn't be there anyway. But she was on some other bullshit at the time, so it was a must he ignore her.

A little later the headliner, Jay V, finally arrived. It was officially show time. Vada's palms got a little sweaty as he thought about what was about to go down. He took shot after shot in an attempt to calm his nerves. This was his big day and he couldn't be anything less than cool.

"Yo," the security guard tapped Jay V on the shoulder only five minutes after he had stepped into the VIP.

"What up?"

"This chick wants to holla at you. She say she know you from New York," the bouncer said while pointing near the velvet ropes to a slim cutie with a big ass booty.

"Let her through," Jay V said.

Although he wasn't interested in the chick for himself, he figured one of the cats from the crew would probably smash. He didn't mind spreading the love. It was all part of the game. Like most rappers, he agreed to listen to what she had to say and hoped she would leave him alone afterwards. The last thing Jay V needed was someone talking his ear off about getting on and passing him a Mix CD.

Vada watched as this thirsty chick spit game to Jay V. She was truly a groupie in motion. He found that shit hilarious. He laughed while throwing back another shot of Patron.

"Here we go," Jay V yelled to Vada while jumping up out of his seat.

Vada heard his intro music. That was a definite sign it was show time. He went straight into performance mode, totally ignoring the groupie that was attempting to talk a hole in his ear.

"If ya'll ready for Jay V to come to the stage let me hear you screammmmmmmmm!!!!!!!" the DJ announced and the crowd roared.

"I can't hear youuuuuuu!!!" he said, and the crowd roared again.

The music to his hit single, Get that Money, blasted out of the music speakers. The crowd went crazy singing along to the song with him. People had their hands and drinks up in the air. Vada fed off the vibe of the crowd. He was getting more and more amp by the second. He knew his time was coming.

"Thank you, thank you for the love and support ya'll have shown me through the years. I can't tell you enough how much it means to a nigga. That's coming from the heart," Jay V expressed then signaled Vada to the stage.

As Vada stood up and headed towards the stage, more of the groupies began eyeing him. He wasn't paying them any mind. He told the bouncer at the rope of the VIP area not let any more of them in.

"I wanna thank everybody for coming out and support-ing me and my label. Without you guys there is no us. Now I want to introduce one of the newest artists to our label. This is Charlotte's very own…Vadaaaaa!" Jay V announced.

While Vada walked on the stage, Jay V pulled out a gold chain with a puppy medallion on it and placed around Vada's neck. They shook hands. The crowd went crazy once again. This sent Vada in overdrive. He was so excited and eager to perform. He grabbed the mic and went on to the music of his new single, Money on my mind.

Me and money got a relationship, we never break up
It's money on my mind every day I wake up
It's rolie on my time, it's time to quake up.

The crowd rocked with Vada the entire performance. After giving a few snippets of some of his hottest songs, Vada's time was up. The crowd loved it and he was loving the vibe from the crowd.

"Nice performance," the big booty groupie from earlier

said to Vada and handed him another shot of Patron as soon as he came off the stage. She realized she was getting nowhere with Jay V, so Vada was now her target.

"Thanks," he said and threw back the shot.

The room was spinning. Vada had one too many drinks.

"You remember...blah, blah, blah." The words the groupie spoke began to run together and Vada had no idea what she was saying.

"Oh, yeah, I remember," he lied.

"Well, I just wanted to say congratulations on your success," she expressed while rubbing his dick.

"Yeah...thanks shortie," Vada said while grabbing her hand, but not removing it.

"Let's go somewhere a little bit quieter." She whispered in his ear then licked the tip of his earlobe.

Vada stood up and began to head out VIP. He was stopped by one of his boys from the crew.

"Yo, Vada, you ain't no ordinary nigga no more. You can't just be walking up out the club alone," his boy said, then grabbed his car keys. "Where you and shortie headed?"

"Take me to my room, cuz. I'm at the Ritz Carlton." Vada said with slurred speech.

Minutes later, Vada was stumbling through the doors of his hotel.

"What's your room number?" the groupie from the club asked.

"Room 205, I think," he said and handed his boy the key. They walked him to the room. Once Vada was in his room safely laid out across the bed, his boy quickly left. The groupie unbuckled Vada's belt and took off his pants and boxers. She grabbed his limp penis and began to stroke it.

"Yo…yo…stop," he requested, pushing the girl away and grabbing his dick.

"You know you want it," she whispered in his ear and took off all of her clothes.

She grabbed his penis that was now erect and began to suck it. This time Vada didn't resist. Now her vagina was soaking wet. She straddled him, glided his dick deep inside her and rode him slowly till both of them came. Soon after, they both fell asleep. The next morning, Vada's phone was blowing up. Out of curiosity, the groupie wanted to see who it was. A picture of a familiar face appeared on the phone. The groupie dropped the phone out of shock. Her heart began to race as she realized what she'd just done.

"Oh shit, I have to get my clothes and get the hell out of here," she said as she scurried around the hotel room. She felt a terrible pain in her stomach. She was overwhelmed with guilt. There weren't many things she regretted in life, but this may have been at the top of her list.

Boom, boom, boom, boom…there was a loud bang on the hotel room door.

"Vada, I can hear that bitch's voice. Let me in here now!" a familiar voice screamed from the other side of the door.

The groupie stood over Vada with her clothes and shoes in her hands. She shoved Vada, "Wake the hell up!" she whispered then ran to the closet. She hid in the closet and squatted down in the corner. Any other woman, she could not have cared less about; however, she and Isis had become close friends and she didn't want to hurt her.

"What's all that banging for?" Vada asked Isis after

opening the door.

"Where is she?" Isis asked, searching everywhere in the room, bathroom and even on the balcony. Lucky for Vada, she didn't open the closet door.

"Ain't nobody in here. I got drunk and fell asleep. I'm putting my clothes on now so we can go home," Vada grabbed his clothes.

"Hurry up," she screamed as she pushed him towards the door.

When she heard the sound of the door shut, Desire let out a sigh of relief. All she wanted was a hot shower and to forget about the entire night.

"Picture Perfect"

Diamond Diva
SERIES

Chapter 7

Victoria

Victoria stared into a tall mirror in her bedroom. She stared at her body, noticing everything that needed improvement. Her breasts needed a pick me up, flabby arms embarrassed her and the cellulite surrounding her legs bothered her. Victoria took a deep breath in disgust. She was on her menstrual cycle and feeling fatter than normal. Her ten-year high school class reunion was coming up and she couldn't dare appear to be anything less than perfect. It was a must that the weight came off and her body got a brand new look.

As much as Victoria hated everything about high school and tried to erase every memory of it, she was the coordinator for the class reunion. As the class president, valedictorian and homecoming queen her senior year, it was only right she planned the reunion. Ten years ago, Victoria was the girl every other high school girl dreamt of being. Victoria closed her eyes and thought back to her senior year in high school. A memory of her mother came to mind.

* * * * *

"My perfect angel is stunning," Victoria's mother, Ruth, said placing her hand on her daughter's shoulder.

She was gazing at Victoria in her Chanel prom dress that was shipped exclusively from New York. Ruth cared about status and name brands. She made sure the "Joneses" were looking up to her family. All throughout her childhood, Victoria was involved in at least three extracurricular activities. Ruth wanted her daughter to become well rounded; however, Victoria felt it just gave her mother something else to brag about to those ladies in her social circle.

"Mom, I'm not feeling well," Victoria expressed.

It was a week after she had been raped.

"Not feeling well? Girl, you better tough it out. This is a chance of a lifetime to attend your prom. Besides, Tom, his parents, and some of my friends are coming by to take pictures. You're a Miller woman. Victoria, you come from a long line of strong women. Now lately, you've been acting a little funny. Whatever you're going through, shake it off. After prom comes graduation and then college. Your father and I didn't work hard for you to be acting crazy now," her mom preached while putting the finishing touches on Victoria's makeup.

Ding dong...The doorbell rang.

"Mom, I need to tell you something..." Victoria began to say with tears in her eyes.

"Not now, whatever it is, it can wait till the weekend is over," Ruth interjected, cutting Victoria off and going to answer the door, not even noticing the pain in her daughters eyes.

DESIRE

* * * * *

After Winston kissed her on the neck, Victoria snapped out of her trip down memory lane. Winston was Victoria's boyfriend. He was "Mr. Perfect". He came from a stellar family—the Vanderhidins—and had graduated top in his class at Morehouse College; majoring in biochemistry. He was tall, gentle, sweet, caring, thought-provoking, handsome and had rock hard abs. His touch made Victoria cringe. This three year relationship was just about going through the motions. Her mother damn near pushed the man on her. His mother and her mother were always in their ears about what they should be and what they needed to do. Ruth adored Winston. The pressure of her mother's expectations was mounting on Victoria, and Winston paid for it in almost every aspect of their relationship.

Winston moved his kiss from the neck to Victoria's lips. Her heart began to race; she knew what was coming next.

"I just want to make love to you," he said before kissing her on the lips again and undressing her.

Victoria let him do whatever he wanted. She figured it would take five minutes for him to take off her clothes and twelve minutes for him to cum. He laid her down on the bed and entered inside of her. Victoria laid there like a lifeless shell. Tears ran down her face as Winston came inside of her. It was dark in the room, so he couldn't see she was crying.

"Thanks, I needed that," Winston said.

"You're welcome. I enjoyed it too," Victoria lied.

"Would you like a glass of wine?" Winston offered.

"No," she shook her head. "I'm going to take a quick shower and then work on some charts I brought home from work."

Victoria took a hot shower. Winston repulsed her. In the shower, she cried to God and asked Him to fix her and give her a better life than the one she had. Victoria demanded to know from God what lesson was to be learned from her getting raped, victimized and not being able to become a mother. She felt God had robbed her of a happy life.

"Cyber Relations"

Diamond Diva
♦♦SERIES♦♦

Chapter 8

Angel

"Baby girl is finally asleep," Sylvester said, coming from the stairs leading into the kitchen.

"She loves story time with Daddy," Angel commented, then giggled while drying the last dish. Angel grew up in a household where using the dishwasher was not allowed and this kitchen rule carried over in her adulthood.

"Honey, do you want a piece of cake?" she offered before leaving the kitchen.

"Of course," he agreed. Sylvester loved Angel's version of moist yellow cake with chocolate frosting.

"I found internet porn on your computer in your office," Angel blabbed out as she handed him the cake.

She not only shocked her husband with that statement, she actually shocked herself. The memory of that night had been haunting her for some time, but she hadn't had the courage to say anything. After speaking with her friend, Isis, it had begun to bother her even more. She'd hoped to just put it all behind her and make it all disappear, but in this case, it looked like God had other plans. Angel was convinced it was the work of the Lord that made her blab that statement out.

"You saw what?" Sylvester said while choking on his cake.

Angel watched as he struggled to catch his breath. She didn't bother to pat his back, get him a sip of water, or any other life-saving mechanism. This may have been God's way of giving him a slap on the wrist and Angel didn't want to interfere with God's work. It took a few minutes for Sylvester to compose himself.

"I don't know want to say."

"Well, for starters, I must warn you. Whatever you do say, don't lie about it," Angel said with her arms crossed.

"I'm sorry. You know my father's history. I vowed not to be like him and I've tried my hardest, but I think I'm beginning to make some poor decisions like him. I didn't want to tell you because I was afraid it was going to scare you away. I wanted to fight this demon alone," Sylvester explained.

"Sylvester, you have never really told me about your father's past. Please tell me more so I can truly understand and look at things from the perspective of your eyes," Angel said rubbing his hand.

Sylvester took a deep breath. "I will try to explain."

"All right, I'm listening." She said in the most supportive manner possible.

"My father and mother were high school sweethearts. For years and years, she overlooked his late nights and not coming home at all for days. Women would come up to her saying that my father was their man, even though my mother had the ring on her finger and a marriage license. On a Sunday afternoon, right after church, mother had heard my father had a baby on the way. He confirmed the rumor and told her it was true. For the rest of the day and night, my mother laid in the bed crying, heartbroken over the news. It hurt me to hear my mother cry that way. My daddy sat me down and told me having lots of women would make me a man. I was ten years old at the time. I vowed to never be like him. My mother never left him, not even after the third child was born. Each child was with a different woman."

"I'm so sorry you and your mother experienced that. She's a good woman."

"Yes, she is and daddy didn't recognize that. He never gave her the love she deserved. He was cold and disconnected. My father was a womanizer to say the least, and I believe some of his ways have trickled down to me," Sylvester admitted.

"You are nowhere near a womanizer, but I do feel you may have some issues we need to address."

"Yes we do. I have certain urges I can't control, Angel." Sylvester confessed.

"Are you addicted to porn, Sylvester?" Angel asked directly, tired of beating around the bush.

"I think so," he shamefully nodded.

"You need to get help." Angel said without delay.

"I want to and will get help."

"Sylvester, I love you. I'm your wife and the mother of your child. It's my Godly duty to stand by you to recover from this addiction. Please keep in mind, you have a daughter that's looking at you and me. I won't have her grow up in a home where that behavior is acceptable."

"I totally understand."

Unlike Sylvester's mother, Angel had her limits. At that point she decided to fast and pray for God to move through their marriage and restore trust. She had vowed before God to be there for better and for worse and she intended on honoring that vow. However, she had one more question for her husband.

"Have you physically been with another woman?"

"No," Sylvester lied, thinking about when Desire went down on him at church.

That night, when Sylvester and Angel said their prayers, he asked for an extra helping of forgiveness from the Lord. Then he and Angel had one last talk before going to bed.

"This needs to stop," she said with her head on her pillow, looking directly in Sylvester's face.

"You're right. May I have your forgiveness?" he asked sincerely.

"Yes, you do; however, it better not happen again. I made an appointment for marriage counseling for next week. I've sacrificed my career and my life for your vision of a church ministry, and I refuse to let it be destroyed because you want to masturbate with a woman in cyberspace. I won't have it," Angel declared.

"I have no objection to that. Maybe the counselor can help me with my porn addiction," Sylvester shamefully said.

"I certainly hope so. Also, I've decided we will be attending the couples' retreat this year at the church. This is one time I think we can benefit."

"Don't you think the church members will think we're having marital issues?" Sylvester questioned his wife on this particular decision.

"Possibly, but no marriage is perfect. And if you want this one to last, you should do whatever it takes to keep it!"

Angel demanded.

"I totally understand. I'm going to fight for this marriage," Sylvester replied, caressing his wife's beautiful face.

"Lingering Lust"

Chapter 9

Desire

" That was an awesome dinner," Desire said as she and Bam walked in her house.

"Yes it was," Bam agreed while rubbing his full stomach.

"It's still early so let's finish the night up by watching a couple movies," Desire said, leading Bam to her bedroom. "Make yourself comfortable." She grabbed the remote and turned on the television. "I'm gonna wash up and change into something a little more comfortable." She headed into the bathroom.

Bam sat on Desires bed and flipped through the channels on the television. There was nothing of interest so he turned to the news. He scanned her room, admiring her décor. She had a California King size bed and lots of modern and eclectic designs and decorations. Bam could immediately tell Desire had expensive taste. He noticed a Bible sitting on the nightstand and wasted no time picking it up. Within minutes he was deep into his reading.

Desire peeped her head out of the bathroom and noticed Bam was on the bed reading something. She had on a white lace lingerie set. They had been hanging out pretty

regularly the past few weeks and she felt it was time to take things to the next level. She crept out of the bathroom on her hands and knees and turned off the light from the lamp that sat on the nightstand. Desire jumped on the bed and pounced onto Bam. She started kissing him and rubbing his dick at the same time.

"Desire, please stop and turn the light back on," Bam calmly suggested.

"You know you want this," she responded, opening her legs and playing with her clit.

"Turn the light back on please, I was reading," Bam requested once again.

"Reading what?" she asked in an irritated tone. Desire wondered what the hell could be more interesting than the gold that lay between her legs.

"I was reading the Bible."

"Fine, read the Bible and enjoy yourself," she said and turned the light back on.

Desire hopped out the bed, rushed to the bathroom, took off the lingerie set and threw it in the dirty clothes hamper. She grabbed an old t-shirt and sweatpants from her dresser drawer, threw them on and headed into the living room. She was horny and did not take rejection well. Dick was easy to find if Bam wasn't willing to fulfill her need. And one thing was for sure, Desire refused to beg any man for dick.

"Wait, Desire, don't go. Let me talk to you for a second," Bam said noticing Desire was upset. "Climb back on the bed," he said while patting an area on the bed next to him.

"No," she said with her arms folded and lips poked out.

Desire was acting like a spoiled brat. She wanted him to beg. The extra attention would make her feel a little better about the rejection she felt.

"Please baby. Come on…don't act like that," Bam's begging was music to Desires ears.

She shook her head no and held the same stance with her arms folded. She didn't budge. She wanted to see just how far Bam would go.

"So that's how you're going to do me?" Bam said in a disappointed tone with a puppy dog face.

Desire finally gave in and climbed on the bed without a response.

"Baby, listen to me," Bam grabbed Desire hands and looked her in the eyes as he spoke. "I want you sexually. I'm sure you know that. Look at you; you're perfect in every way. Any man would be crazy not to be attracted to you. But I've made certain decisions in life and I have to stand by them," Bam tried explaining.

"Decisions? What you mean? Don't tell me you're celibate!" Desire spat.

"Well, yeah. That is one of the decisions I've made. I'm not having sex until I'm married," Bam said sincerely.

Desire didn't respond. She just gave Bam a blank stare. She didn't know if this fool was seriously that strong about his religion or if he was just plain old gay and using religion for an excuse. She knew something had to be wrong for him to turn her down in the bed. That was unheard of!

"I have a very deep relationship with God and nothing comes between that, not even sex. I've made a lot of bad choices in my past and I am certain it's only by the grace and mercy of God I'm still here." Bam tried not to sound like he was preaching a church sermon, but he needed Desire to understand his situation.

"Oh, yeah? Like what kind of bad choices?" Desire asked, more interested in his past instead of all that God stuff he was talking about.

"In high school I did some terrible things and it only got worse once it got drafted into the NFL," Bam began to explain before being interrupted by Desire.

"NFL? I never knew you played profession football!" she said full of excitement.

"Yeah, but it was a very short spin. I got hurt after only a few seasons and never fully recovered. Before I knew it, I was a bench rider and addicted to painkillers. I guess I was trying to dull the pain of feeling like a failure. Eventually, I was dropped and that's when I hit rock bottom. I had gone from rich and famous to broke and alone. I had begun selling myself to rich women just to keep a little money in my pocket and to have a little companionship. I felt less than a man," Bam explained.

"Wow! That's crazy!" Desire couldn't believe what she was hearing.

"Yeah. It didn't take long for my crazy ways to catch up with me though. Eventually, I landed in jail, and that's where my life turned around."

"Really?" Desire responded, now a little more intrigued by the conversation. She felt like she could relate to what Bam had gone through.

"When I was locked up, I would always attend the church service. There was nothing else to do so I went to pass time.

Plus, I thought it would look good when it was time for release. One day a preacher came in and told me that God loved me and He forgave me. I'll never forget it because it was almost as if a white light was shining on him as he was telling me."

"I know exactly what you mean," Desire admitted. She was really tuned in to the conversation. It brought back memories of when she was in jail. It was Isis that convinced her to attend church and look towards God for all things. Her heart began to ache as she thought about the night she betrayed her friend by sleeping with Vada.

"Do you?" Bam caressed Desires face gently.

"Yes. I do know the Lord, you know? It's just life's experiences that have changed my ways," Desire explained.

"Desire, look at me." He looked her directly in the eyes. "I really like you as a person and for your heart, not for the tricks you can do in the bedroom. In the past you may have used sex to get what you wanted. That is not necessary with me. You're beautiful inside and out." He kissed her gently.

Desire's eyes filled with tears and she had a big lump in her throat. It took everything in her to hold back the tears. What Bam was saying was the truth and the truth hurt.

"I want you in my life, but I need you to walk the same path as me," Bam said sincerely.

"So how can I do that?" Desire asked.

"Well, for starters, I read the Bible to get a closer relationship with God. This time is important to me. I would like to share that time with you."

"Okay," Desire readily agreed.

"Let's bow our heads and pray," Bam said as he gently

took her hands.

"God, we come before you today as two people who have both had turbulent pasts. It's not where you come from; it's where you're going. God, You are leader of our lives. Let Your will be done. Desire and I love You and give our hearts, minds and souls to You. Thank You for healing the past and renewing our lives." He paused then asked Desire, "Is there anything you would like to add?"

"Ummm…I just want to ask for forgiveness," Desire added.

She didn't want to elaborate. She figured if God was a knowing God, then He knew what she needed forgiveness for.

"Okay. Well, that concludes our prayer. In Jesus name, we pray, Amen."

After that night, Desire had a new found respect for Bam.

"Good morning," Desire said to Bam as he awakened to breakfast which included a Belgian waffle, grits, bacon and scrambled eggs with cheese.

"Thank you," he said smiling.

"You're welcome, enjoy your day. I'm going to head to the salon. You can see yourself out. Lock the bottom lock when you leave." Desire grabbed her purse and keys.

"Before you go, there's a couples' weekend retreat coming up soon. I would like for us to go," he expressed.

"When is it?"

"Next weekend."

"Okay," Desire responded.

She wasn't sure what the retreat was all about, but it was time alone with Bam and that's all that mattered.

"Time for a Vacation"

Diamond Diva
SERIES

G STREET CHRONICLES
A LITERARY POWERHOUSE
WWW.GSTREETCHRONICLES.COM

Chapter 10

Isis

It was Sunday afternoon and Isis had a massive hangover. She had spent the previous night bar hopping with her girls in a desperate attempt to get rid of the "boyfriend blues". Her and Vada's relationship was on the rocks and she wasn't quite sure where it would end.

The phone had been ringing off the hook. It took at least three calls back to back before she decided to even look at the caller ID. Isis figured if someone had called that many times it had to be some sort of an emergency, but to her surprise it was Angel. Isis began to worry. She figured something bad must have happened for her to call on a Sunday afternoon. That was usually her after-church family time.

"Hello," Isis answered the phone, wondering if Angel had finally caught Sylvester's ass doing dirt.

"Happy Sunday!" Angel sang into the phone.

"Yeah, yeah. What's so happy about it?" Isis grumbled.

"God has allowed you to see another day," she began to preach.

"Okay, okay," Isis said interrupting her. She was not in the mood for a sermon. If she wanted to hear the Word she

would have gotten her drunken ass up and gone to church her damn self.

"So what is going on that you had to call so many times back to back?" Isis asked her friend.

"Uuummm…this is my first phone call, honey. But I do have some good news!"

"Oh, really? What is it?" Isis asked, kind of eager to hear what she had to say.

"The church is planning a couples' retreat. Sylvester and I are going and I think you and Vada should come too. It'll be so much fun. I'm sure you could use a break from the kids," Angel explained.

"Oh, I don't know," Isis began to say.

"I will not take no for an answer. I've already purchased the packages," Angel said totally cutting Isis off.

She began to think. A break from those kids did sound like a good idea. "Where is the retreat being held?" she inquired.

"Poconos!" Angel said full of excitement.

"Oh, I'm down!" Isis said right away.

No more contemplating was necessary after hearing the location. She knew she would never have an opportunity to take a paid-in-full trip like that again. There was no way she was turning that trip down.

"Great! We leave next weekend."

"Next weekend? That's really short notice." Isis said, knowing it would be impossible to get a babysitter on such short notice.

"It's okay. I've got everything covered. If you're worried about childcare, the church is providing childcare for all the couples participating."

Angel had it all mapped out. There was no way Isis could get out of this one, so she gave in without a fight. She was looking forward to a vacation, but not so much with Vada. Their relationship had been on the rocks ever since he'd gotten his new record deal and Isis wasn't feeling him at all. Maybe this trip was exactly what they needed to rekindle things.

* * * * *

"So you got me in the wilderness for what now?" Vada asked as they were pulling up to the cabin.

"Don't get me started, Vada. You know exactly what you did. That's why you have been letting me blow up that credit card of yours. I really thought you were lying when you said your card had no limit," Isis replied while pulling down the mirror on the passenger side of the vehicle to make sure nothing was stuck in between her teeth. She wanted to look her best when she stepped out the car and faced the "church folk."

"I didn't do anything." Vada shook his head denying the allegations. "I gave you the black card so you could buy yourself something nice. It's been a while since I've given my special lady something special," Vada caressed Isis cheek then attempted to give her a small peck on the lips.

"Eh eh." Isis pulled back. "You're gonna mess up my lipstick," she said taking another glance at herself in the mirror.

Vada didn't respond. He just looked as his wife and gave a subtle smile. With the constant fussing and fighting, he had forgotten how beautiful she was. Guilt rattled his mind. Even though, Vada didn't remember much, he could recall that chick being on top of him. Vada just wanted all the negativity to go away. He had a wife, kids and a new record label that prided on their artists behaving to some degree. If this retreat and shopping sprees would appease Isis, then so be it. Vada took a deep breath, hoping to get through the weekend without any craziness.

"I'm going to get the bags from the trunk," Vada said.

"All right," Isis agreed while getting out of the car and taking her sunglasses off.

"Welcome." Minister Biles and his wife, Jennifer, greeted them at the door.

"Hello," Isis said, coming closer and shaking their hands.

Vada followed behind her and did the same thing with five bags on his arms. He couldn't understand why Isis needed so much luggage. They were only going away for the weekend. No matter where Isis went, even if it was going to the store, she always had to look her best.

As she walked up, Isis noticed two other couples were already there mingling with each other in the other room.

"I'm sorry, are we late?" Isis asked Jennifer while looking at the time on her brand new Brighton watch.

"Just a little, honey; however, it's all right. We have approximately one hundred couples here today, so we have fallen a little behind ourselves. We have separated everyone into teams of three couples each. This provides a more intimate setting and individualized attention." She explained, and then continued, "We'll give you a few minutes to get settled. Your suite is upstairs; the first room to the left where you'll find fresh green towels on the dresser. There are re-freshments in the meeting room if you would like a snack before we get started in thirty minutes."

"All right," Vada and Isis agreed in unison before walking upstairs.

"You can't be on time for anything," Vada griped as he placed the bags on the carpet in the bedroom.

It was a quaint bedroom that Isis felt comfortable in. She completely ignored Vada's comment as she made her way to the bathroom to relieve herself. She knew he didn't realize that having two small children, getting them fed, dressed and whisked off to the babysitter was a task. Thirty minutes is nothing compared to some other tardy appearances in the past. Isis popped a piece of Wrigley's gum in her mouth, took a quick glance in the mirror and headed to the door.

"Let's go, I'm ready to save this marriage. Tomorrow may be a different story," Isis said.

"Baby, I didn't do anything with anyone. I assure you. Did you see another woman in the room?" Vada asked while placing his arm around her waist and pulling her close to him.

"Nope. Maybe because the skank left before I could catch the two of you in a sexual act. God knows how much I could have taken. You would have died that day and I would have gotten away with the murder charges." She gave a small smirk then kissed him on the lips.

They both headed downstairs to the meeting room to meet the other couples. Isis noticed the petits fours on the table. She made a mental note to grab one before heading to bed. Isis and Vada started mingling with the other couples on their designated team. Out the corner of her eye she saw a familiar face. She couldn't believe who she was seeing as she walked closer.

"Desire," Isis screamed and ran over to her long lost friend for a hug.

"Where have you been?" Desire asked with tears in her eyes.

"I lost my phone and had no way to contact you. I have been going through it with my husband," she mumbled under her breath so only Desire could hear.

"We can't ever lose touch again," Isis said. They both agreed while placing their contact numbers and email addresses into each other's smart phones.

Isis then began to introduce Desire to everyone, starting with her significant other. "This is my husband, Vada."

Vada took a glance at Desire then took a double take as if he remembered her from the romp in the hotel room.

Desire's heart sunk to her stomach when she saw Vada. "The infamous Vada...I've heard a lot about you." She tried to act normal and not look too guilty. Desire was cool. As long as he played it off, so would she. The last thing she wanted to do was hurt Isis. Isis may have been the only friend she had.

Next Isis introduced Desire to Angel. "This is my long-time friend, Angel. We've been besties since high school. She is married to Bishop Sylvester Rollins."

"Nice to meet you," Desire said extending her hand.

Desire, Angel and Isis had a little bit of small talk. Desire realized Angel wasn't so bad after all and under different circumstances maybe they could have been friends.

"Well, hello again, everyone, let's get started. I'm John Biles and this is Jennifer, my wife of thirty two years, who has been by my side for the ups and downs of the roller coaster ride called marriage. We both are licensed professional counselors with extensive experience in couple's therapy. We will be you team leaders this weekend. Let's take our seats and introduce ourselves around the room and state why you are here."

After each person around the room introduced themselves, stating a little background on their lives, Minister Biles took over.

"Let's bow our heads and pray," he instructed the group. "Dear, Lord, thank You for my wife and these couples who were courageous enough to attend this retreat to enhance their marriage. Lord, we know that You honor marriage and the vows. Bless each and every one here today in Jesus name, Amen."

After the prayer, the couples helped themselves to refreshments and mingled a bit. Isis began to get a bad feeling in her stomach. A smell lingered in the air and it was way too familiar. She knew exactly where it was coming from. It was Desire. It was the same perfume that Desire had on when she was thrown into jail. She always talked about the scent called Aqua, it was rather expensive and the only perfume that she sprayed on her neck and clothes. It was the same scent that was in the hotel room the morning she caught Vada. All sorts of things began to pop in Isis's mind as she watched Vada and Desire closely.

"So now, let's get started; it's time for open dialogue. Tell us why you came here and what you hope to accomplish this weekend." Minister Bile's words seem to be at a distance to Isis who was deep thought.

"My husband cheated on me with that back-stabbing bitch, Desire!" Isis screamed.

She punched Vada in the face then kicked him in the balls. Isis grabbed a knife from the kitchen and snatched Desire's hair and pushed her up against the wall.

"Nooooo!!!!!! Put the knife down," she could hear someone yelling.

"This isn't the answer," another added.

"Stabbing her isn't the answer," someone else screamed.

"In prison, when no one wanted to be your friend, I was there for you one hundred and ten percent. After everything we have been through, this is how you repay me? You sleep with my husband? I knew by your infamous perfume. It's the same stench that was in the hotel room that morning," she said while nicking Desire's neck with the knife.

"Isis...Isis!" Vada was shaking Isis by the arm.

"Yes. What is it?" Isis asked snapping out of her terror daydream.

"It's your turn to speak, bae. The minister has been talking to us for the past five minutes."

Isis looked up to see everyone in the room staring at her. Her face felt flush with embarrassment.

"Couples' Retreat"

Chapter 11

Desire

It was day two of the couples' retreat and Desire was truly enjoying it. This day was all about pressuring people to get what she wanted. She made it her personal mission to pressure the bishop into paying her the money he owed, and pressuring Bam into letting her get a taste of his sexy chocolate. Desire felt the atmosphere was perfect for love making and she would be able to work her magic on him.

Bam and Desire met the other couples in the meeting room for breakfast. As she sat eating, Desire realized she'd had some sort of sexual relations with half of the men that were in the room at the time. Even with that realization hanging over her, she still played it cool with the other couples. She already made it up in her mind if either one of those niggas spilled their hearts out about their indiscretions with her, she would make sure those two would go down with her. Things had really grown between her and Bam and she wasn't taking any chances at losing his heart. Desire was really feeling him. She hadn't opened her heart to a man in a long time, but was willing to try her hand at love with Bam. However, that lifestyle of fast money still would always be

her first love. Desire really wanted those spirits of lust and greed bound and released out of her through prayer, but she knew it would take a long hard journey before she got to that point.

Desire glanced across the table at the bishop. From the looks of things, her mere presence was making him uncomfortable. He couldn't stop sweating. Knowing he could be in the hot seat terrified him. He knew at this point, Desire was so close to ruining his life. He also knew from the way Angel spoke to him the night of their conversation, she meant business. The way things were going, Sylvester wasn't even sure if she could forgive him and still stay married to him if she found out the truth about him and Desire. The last thing he wanted was a divorce. Not only did he hate the thought of losing his wife and child, but he knew if he did under those circumstances, it would permanently cripple his ministry.

"Sylvester, are you all right?" Desire watched as his wife questioned him after noticing his strange behavior.

"Yes, those ribs from the Shed restaurant last night didn't sit well with my stomach. Coming off a five day fast and eating ribs wasn't the smartest idea. I'll be fine," he lied.

After breakfast, the bishop excused himself to the restroom to text Desire. The stress and anxiety was killing him. He offered eight thousand dollars to be done and finished with her. He couldn't take the pressure any longer. The bishop was pacing the bathroom floor waiting to get a reply from Desire. A few minutes later, she responded:

I want ten thousand dollars, plus an extra five hundred for fucking with me. . .or that perfect little life you're living will come to a quick end.

He caved in and did exactly as Desire instructed. With a click of a button on his cell phone he did a wire transfer from his personal bank account to hers. Then he texted her to notify her the transaction was complete. A few minutes later, Desire replied back:

I have received the money. You may now come back to the group.

Desire wanted to jump up and shout for joy. She didn't expect the bishop to fold so easily. She excused herself from the group and headed to the lobby area for a little privacy. She transferred the money the bishop had wired to another bank account to ensure its safety. Even though wire transfers couldn't be reversed, Desire wanted to ensure the safety of the money. In her eyes, she deserved every penny of it. Fulfilling men's fantasies was hard work. Desire returned to the meeting room to join the others. This time when glancing at the bishop, he looked calm and relaxed. She gave him a mischievous smirk, then headed towards Bam.

"Let's ditch the group today and have a little fun of our own," she whispered in his ear.

"Okay," Bam agreed, surprising Desire.

Desire was excited as they headed back to their suite. Her day was going easier than planned. As she walked out of the meeting room she heard her name called.

"Hey!" she said noticing it was Isis.

"We need to talk. There has been something on my mind," Isis said, pulling Desire aside.

"I'm all ears," Desire nervously said. She was praying Vada hadn't broken down and told Isis they had sex.

"Do you know my husband from somewhere?" Isis didn't bother beating around the bush.

"You know what? I can't even lie to you," Desire paused and took a deep breath. "Yes, I do."

"Oh, really? Would like to tell me about it?" Isis crossed her arms and stepped closer to Desire.

Although Isis was approaching her in a threatening manner, Desire really didn't want to take it there. First of all, she wasn't trying to fight someone she considered a friend. Secondly, she wasn't even the fighting type. She would much rather make love or get money.

"I met him a week ago at the club," she said, giving the least amount of information. She wasn't sure how much Isis really knew, so she wanted to tread lightly.

"Okay and…" Isis said knowing there was more to the story.

"And I left with him after the club," Desire admitted.

"So you had sex with my husband?" Isis said calmly.

"Please Isis, let me explain—"

Smack! Isis backhanded Desire in the face before she had a chance to even finish her sentence.

"Yo!" Bam grabbed Isis, preventing her from getting to Desire.

"If you knew why I smacked her, you wouldn't be holding me back right now," Isis yelled.

Vada rushed over and tackled Bam to the ground. The bishop grabbed Bam and Minister Biles grabbed Vada. Desire stood motionless, in disbelief. Her brain was racing. She couldn't believe things had gone left so quickly.

"Upstairs now!" Bam grabbed Desire by the arm and pushed her towards the stairs.

"Baby can we talk?" Desire asked as soon as they walked

in their private suite.

Bam didn't even respond. He just looked at her, shock his head, and got undressed. Desire knew she was in trouble and had some making up to do, so she figured she would do what she knew best…use her sex appeal. Besides, seeing his perfect, naked body instantly turned her on. Her mind was yelling, *no bitch, he's mad,* but her pussy was soaking wet and shivering like a nympho feigning over the last piece of dick. *And we all know when it comes to a feign, the mind never wins.* So like a nympho, Desire got undressed and followed Bam into the shower.

"What are you doing, Desire," Bam asked as she hugged him gently from the back.

"Ssshhhh…" Desire whispered as she kissed him on the neck.

"Don't do this," he said as he calmly removed her hands from his chest.

"Baby I need to feel you inside me," Desire begged as she rubbed his penis.

Desire knew no man could resist the long strokes of her wet, soapy hand against their penis. She knew once he was hard she was definitely gonna get some.

"Desire, don't do this!" Bam said with a tad bit of aggression.

"Really, Bam?" Desire asked, questioning his anger.

"Really," he said as he stepped out the shower and grabbed his towel.

Desire couldn't believe Bam. She had never met a man who could turn down her stuff like he did. She knew he was all Godly and loved his religion and all, but at the time, she really didn't give a fuck. She was crazy horny and needed some relief. Realizing she wasn't gonna get that relief from Bam, she did what she had to do. Desire leaned against the shower wall, propped one leg on the side of the tub, and positioned the shower head perfectly so that the water flowed across her breast and clit. Then she closed her eyes and placed her fingers between her legs giving her clit a gentle massage. Her legs got weak as she began to reach her peak.

"Ah, uumm, ahh…" Desire yelled out as she released.

She could see the silhouette of Bam's body as she came. He was at the sink brushing his teeth.

"I'm a woman that can please herself," Desire laughed, then finished washing up.

"Marriage Counselor"

Chapter 12

Angel

After arriving home from the retreat, Angel laid on her bed feeling refreshed. She thanked God for the private time she had with her husband and the counseling they received from Minister Biles. Now Angel truly had faith she and Sylvester could get past their struggle and she was confident her marriage would last after all.

She wished she could say the same for her bestie. She felt bad for Isis, but she was grateful not to be in her shoes. The heartbreak, betrayal, and humiliation would have been too much for Angel to handle. Sylvester was fast asleep. After going downstairs to make a cup of green tea, she wanted to give Isis a ring.

"Hey, girl," Isis said sound groggy.

"Did I catch you at a bad time?"

"No, you didn't. I was just putting my son down for the night. Then, I'm heading to bed shortly."

"Oh, okay. I won't keep you long. I just wanted to thank you for coming to the retreat. I think it was a huge success!"

"A huge success for who, Angel?" Isis said with a bit of aggravation in her tone.

"Well, I would say for everyone."

"So you think me finding out my husband cheated with my best friend was a success? Are you serious right now?" Isis snapped.

"No not at all. However, I do think the fact that you all were able to find out the truth was a step in the right direction. Now you guys can work on repairing, like Sylvester and I have." Angel tried explaining.

"Listen honey, there is no repairing going on around here. That retreat has ruined my damn marriage! I kicked Vada out of the house. I'm truly hurting, right now. I gave this man everything and it's still not enough because he has to fuck bitches behind my back! I've been crying since we left the retreat. His sorry ass isn't worth my tears. I know he isn't, but it hurts so bad!" Isis screamed through the phone.

"Let's pray. We learned from Minister Biles that we need to pray even harder at times like this," Angel suggested, remembering the tools to a successful marriage they learned while at the retreat.

"Angel, I'm not in the mood for you tonight. I can't do this. God hasn't been in my house for some time now and I don't think He is coming tonight either. So let's not pray!"

"You're upset. I understand, but, your marriage can be restored. You're speaking out of emotion right not. You're not thinking logically, Isis."

"Angel..." Isis giggled after saying her name.

"What's so funny?"

"You are. In fact, you're hilarious. The joke has been on you and for a long time, honey."

"What are you talking about?" Angel inquired.

"Wake the fuck up, Angel, and stop being so damn naïve. When you tied the knot at that extravagant wedding of yours to Sylvester, you lost all common sense. The world isn't as great as you think it is. Sylvester has been sleeping with women behind your back for years. This porno mess on the internet isn't the worst he's ever done," Isis spat.

"What? Where is all this coming from? How long have you known these things?" Angel asked in total shock.

"There's no point in us going there because I'm not going to listen to you try to convince yourself about how it's not true and how you don't believe me. It's like I don't even know you anymore. You are not the best friend I grew up with and loved. I'm tired and I have my own fucking problems. Good night," Isis stated then hung up on Angel.

Angel immediately called her back. The phone went straight to voicemail. She tried several more times, but it was the same. She even tried calling her house phone, but even then she got voicemail. Angel was totally blown away by the way her best friend had just lashed out at her. She was confused and hurt. Funny thing is, she had no anger towards her at all. The average person would have been livid by Isis's actions, but not Angel, God had put her in a different place.

The kettle whistled as an indication that the water was hot. Angel prepared her tea and walked upstairs in disbelief. The devil was getting in her head. As she thought about the things Isis said about Sylvester cheating, her mind began to swarm with past occurrences that she should have picked up on. When she reached her bedroom, she stood at the foot of the bed and stared at her husband. For a split second an evil presence came over her and she thought of gently unfolding the covers off Sylvester and pouring the hot cup of tea all over his face. Quickly she snapped out of it and placed the covers back on her husband and put the tea cup on the nightstand. Angel knew the devil was trying her and she needed to pray. So without hesitation she got down on her knees and quietly asked God for forgiveness for playing into the devil's hand and for strength to fight the tricks of the devil. She rebuked the spirits of jealously, anger, and vengeance in Jesus name and ended her prayer. Within moments, a peaceful presence filled her. She got in bed and hugged her husband tightly. An oblivious Sylvester reached over and snuggled with his wife.

"It's all an Illusion"

Chapter 13

Victoria

Another night of being fake had become exhausting for Victoria. Life with Winston and maintaining her polished appearance was becoming more and more of an acting role every day. Victoria found it ironic how the couple that was envied the most by everyone around them, was the same couple that was crumbling behind closed doors. Nonetheless, she put on her fake smile and hopped in the car with her partner by her side. They were headed to the Westin Hotel where her high school reunion was being held. Preparing and planning this event had grasped her life for the past six months. Victoria was relieved that the day of her class reunion had finally come and would and soon be over. Victoria promised herself that she wouldn't commit to another league or club for a while. Those actions were following in her mother's footsteps. Those were the things her mother loved; but Victoria wanted to be her own person.

After pulling up to the hotel valet, Winston and Victoria grasped hands and headed into the hotel. As they entered into the ballroom, Victoria immediately began to recognize familiar faces. She said hello to a few people before heading

to the picture area. After taking a formal picture, Winston went to the bar to grab a couple glasses of wine. Victoria used this as an opportunity to mingle with other people.

"So, how has life been treating you? Are you married? Any kids? What kind of work do you do?" Everyone was asking the exact questions that Victoria had predicted. Victoria had already rehearsed her responses to the questions. Although the story she told people was far from the truth, she gave the impression that she had the picture-perfect life they all expected. Her fronts were up in portraying that she was actually happy.

"Victoria?" A woman called her name as she approached, just as she was finishing her conversation with another class-mate.

The familiar face stood before her with a huge smile and looked as though she wanted to hug Victoria tightly. Unfortunately, the feelings weren't mutual. Victoria didn't expect to see her at the reunion. After all, she never even attended her high school.

"Hello," Victoria said while smiling, and then took a sip of her white wine hoping the conversation wouldn't go any further.

"It's good to see you," her old friend hugged her tight.

"Likewise, Desire," Victoria lied.

"So, do you still live in the area?"

"Yes." Victoria nodded.

"I heard that you were delivering babies at the hospital. I always knew you would be a doctor. It's truly the only thing you talked about."

"Yes, that's right, but I'm a physician assistant," she

corrected her. People always mistook Victoria for a doctor. "How are things going with you?" she switched the conversation off of her and on to Desire.

"Great! I did move away for a little while and then came back. I just can't leave Charlotte!"

"I totally understand." Victoria went along with the small talk.

"I'm in the process of opening a high-end salon and spa. You should come by and check it out once I'm established," Desire suggested.

"Will do. So tell me, what are you doing at this reunion? You didn't go to school here," Victoria inquired.

"I'm on a date. I'm here with that man at the bar. He graduated with you. Maybe you know him. He was the star football player, his name is…"

"Bam," Victoria finished Desire's sentence.

A ton of emotions rushed through Victoria. Her body felt warm and she was a bit dizzy.

"Yes! He's a wonderful guy. I consider myself lucky to have found someone like him," Desire rambled on, but Victoria was zoned out since she spoke the name Bam.

She began to pant. She felt as though she couldn't catch her breath. She started shaking uncontrollably. Victoria was having a full-blown panic attack.

"Excuse me for a moment, I need to go to…" Victoria tried to explain her sudden nausea while pointing to the nearest bathroom. She rushed off before finishing her sentence. When she got to the bathroom, she quickly found a stall. She made it just in time to release the vomit that was rushing out. A moment later would have been too late. She thanked God she made it. The last thing Victoria wanted was to make a scene and possible ruin her squeaky-clean reputation.

Are you all right?" Desire asked after chasing behind her.

"Yes, I think I caught a stomach bug," Victoria said while taking deep breaths.

"I will be right back with a ginger ale to help settle your stomach."

Several minutes passed, as Victoria waited for Desire. She was grateful that no one else came into the bathroom.

"Here you go," Desire said after returning and handing a small can of ginger ale to Victoria.

"Thank you," Victoria replied, and then took a few sips.

"You're welcome."

"What a night," Victoria stated while finishing up her drink. Her stomach was finally settled and she felt a whole lot better. She reached in her purse for the travel-size toothbrush and toothpaste she always carried. After brushing her teeth she touched up her makeup and prepared to return to the class reunion.

"Are you sure that you have a stomach bug? Maybe, you're prego," Desire giggled.

"Maybe, I am. Winston and I will be picking up a few home pregnancy tests on the way home," Victoria joked along.

"Yes, that would be a good idea. Can I get you anything else?"

"No, I'm fine. Desire, go have a good time. I don't want to ruin your evening."

"You're not ruining my evening. I'm going back into the

ballroom. Let me know if I can help you in anyway. The buffet is loaded with food, but I did notice some crackers near the salad bar. That might go better with the ginger ale."

"Okay. Thanks again," Victoria said after applying her lipstick.

When she heard the bathroom door close behind Desire, she began to sob. It had been ten years since she saw Bam. Although the day of her rape haunted her mind on a daily basis, the sight of him brought back all sorts of overwhelming feelings.

"Home Run"

Chapter 14

Desire

Desire loved soaking in a hot bubble bath. It was the time of the day that brought her the most relaxation. As she slipped into the bath she'd just prepared, she closed her eyes and began to think about how her life had changed so quickly. Less than a year ago, she was unwillingly clung to a jail cell with only a dream that she and Isis talked about on a daily basis. Now, that dream had become a reality.

She never planned on coming home and joining an on-line porn site. And she definitely never planned on giving head to a prominent bishop; however, she did specialize in hustling men for money. In this case, she put that hustle to good use because the business was finally starting to break ground. Desire was confident that in a few more months, the salon and spa would begin making a large profit. The bishop's money and Bam's constant praying, encouragement, handiwork and support, all played a huge part in getting the business up and running.

Desire had a lot to be thankful for and she knew it. She never expected a man like Bam to come along. He was an absolute gentleman. He opened doors and gave bouquets

of flower and Edible arrangements—just because. Desire began to wonder if she had finally met Mr. Right. No man had ever made Desire want to settle down and do the right things in life. She found herself thinking about Bam before making any decision. She was in church every Sunday and praying had become part of her daily routine. Being with Bam had really changed her. Although she shared no intimacy with him, their intimacy with God had enhanced their relationship. Desire was starting to give her heart to Bam and totally trust him.

After the retreat, things were a little rough, but Bam finally got over it and they were on the right path. Although she had lost her best friend, Isis, she'd gained her old best friend, Victoria. Life wasn't perfect, but it sure was improving by leaps and bounds.

"Hello there," Desire said as Bam stepped into the bathroom.

"Hi baby," he said, then walked closer to give her a kiss on the cheek. Desire loved those soft pecks.

"Take your clothes off and come in. The water is still hot. You look as though you had a long day," she said, revealing her breasts which rose above the bubbles.

"Good idea and I did," Bam said while taking his clothes off.

Once he was fully undressed, Desire noticed his dick was hard. Some nights, she would tests the limits with Bam just to see how far she could go before he would say stop. Desire had never met a man that could resist her sexual advances, so Bam was definitely a challenge. He placed his back against the oval-shaped tub and Desire placed herself against his chest. Bam grabbed the body wash and a sponge and started bathing her. She loved his gentle touch.

"You look happy. Tell me what's on your mind?" Bam said, noticing the look of total bliss on his girlfriend's face.

"I'm just so happy. Everything in my life is finally coming together. I have a wonderful man and I'm finally reaching my goals," Desire said sincerely.

"I told you with God all things are possible, baby. You just have to align your life with His will."

"I know. I'm so glad you came into my life." Desire gave Bam a kiss on the lips then continued to talk about her day. "I'm getting excited about the grand opening of the salon. I got my business cards and invitations today. I'm going to invite all my girls, especially the ones from high school. Of course, I'm going to invite Isis and Victoria. Isis was my motivation to make all this happen and Victoria has been my bestie since I was a teenager."

Bam instantly sat up slightly pushing Desire away from him.

"What's wrong, babe?" she asked, noticing a sudden change in his energy.

"The water is getting cold. I'm going to run more hot water," he said while reaching for the faucet.

"What else? That's not it," Desire said. She knew her man and it was obvious he was bothered by something.

"Well, Desire…" Bam paused then continued, "I'm not really cool with you hanging out with Victoria. That girl is bad news. I can't explain why I feel that way, but my spirit just doesn't accept her. Listen to me; I know people's character…keep your distance from her," Bam pleaded.

"But why? I mean, you just can't tell me to stay away from my best friend and expect me to agree."

"Trust me. In public, people are one way. In private, they are another way. Let's just say I've heard rumors."

"Rumors? Victoria is just as her name states, prestige. She graduated top of her class in high school and in college when she received her Master's degree. Not to mention, she was homecoming queen and comes from a very respectable family. She and her dude seem in a blissful place with a picture-perfect life. So I don't know what rumors you could have heard." Desire defended her friend.

"I'm not going to get into all that. Desire, I have been working nonstop. The last thing I want to do is talk about other people. I brought dinner from Outback for us. Let's just enjoy the night. Okay?" Bam suggested, ending the conversation.

"Okay," Desire said, then shrugged her shoulders.

Bam climbed out of the tub, grabbed a towel from the counter and started drying himself off. Desire admired his perfect body. His chest was impeccable and hairless. Desire didn't like hair on a man's chest. His legs were chiseled, sturdy broad shoulders and his arm muscles he wrapped around her body were ripped. Most of all, Desire adored Bam's smile. She watched his every move and daydreamed about what it would be like to have sex with him.

"Ouch!" she screamed out.

A stomach pain similar to a cramp interrupted her thoughts. The room started to spin just a bit. Desire figured she may have been feeling that way because she'd been sitting in a hot tub for too long. So she gathered herself and stepped out the tub.

As Bam was about to walk out of the bathroom, he turned around and stared at Desire. Suddenly, he started walking back to her. Bam started kissing Desire. Their tongues touched. Desire hopped on the sink and opened her legs. Bam began to lotion her entire body, rubbing her feet and ending at the nape of her neck. His tongue played with her earlobes. Desire pushed his head towards her breast. To her surprise he licked her nipples. Her vagina instantly became flooded with her juices. Desire pushed Bam's head down further, and his kisses followed down her stomach. She moaned as she gave him one more small shove, landing his head between her legs. She leaned back against the mirror and spread her legs wide, welcoming his tongue into her pussy.

"Aaaaaah," she moaned, releasing her cum into his mouth. Bam swallowed every ounce of her wetness. Moments later, Bam stood up. He washed his face and brushed his teeth without even looking at Desire.

"Meet me downstairs so we can eat. I picked up your favorite," he said as he walked out the bathroom.

Desire sat on the bathroom counter and leaned against the mirror in amazement. She couldn't believe she'd finally had sexual activity with Bam. She would have much rather had his penis inside her, but she was happy with oral sex. At least it was a step in the right direction. A few minutes later, she got up and began to get dressed. She grabbed her favorite jeans and slid them on. They seem a little snug as she pulled them over her hips, but when she attempted to button them she couldn't. She couldn't even suck and tuck to get the button to close. She gave up and tried another pair, only to have the same issue. She totally gave up on jeans and threw on a nice casual dress and a cute pair of heels and headed downstairs.

"The food looks great," Desire commented as she entered the kitchen.

When she sat down, her stomach started to turn. She felt nauseous, but didn't want to tell Bam. She took a few deep breaths and regrouped. As the waves of nausea subsided, Desire decided to take another peak at the plate of a fully loaded baked potato, medium-well filet mignon, tender grilled shrimp, and a crisp salad.

"Thanks, baby. What a wonderful surprise!" Desire said feeling relaxed. That orgasm was exactly what she needed to relieve some of the built up stress and tension she'd been feeling.

"You're welcome," Bam said before taking a bite of his salad.

There was a brief silence in the room. Bam decided to focus on the television which had the highlights of a football game from the night before. Honestly, he felt bad for having oral sex with Desire. Even though he did want her so bad, Bam wanted to wait until their wedding night to have any type of sexual relations with her. Also, he felt bad about the thoughts that flashed through his head. While having Desire's nipple in his mouth, he was secretly thinking about Victoria. He had mixed feelings of hate and fascination with Victoria; however, his heart truly belonged to Desire. Bam was at a loss for words and didn't know what to say to Desire. All he wanted to do was eat and curl up in bed with her.

"Bam…Bam…Hellooooo…Bam," Desire repeated until getting his attention.

"Huh? Yes, baby?"

"Wow, you must have been deep in thought. I just told you that I saw a cat with wings on my way home."

"I'm sorry baby. I haven't exactly been listening to you this entire time," Bam admitted.

"I can tell. You have something on your mind?" Desire asking, knowing that Bam probably felt some sort of way about what just happened.

"No, sweetheart. Everything is fine," he said, not even making eye contact with her.

"Mmm hhmmm. I know you feel bad for going down on me. It's my fault," Desire blabbed out. She knew Bam would never just come out and admit what was bothering him.

"How is your fault?" Bam finally lifted his head and made eye contact with Desire. "I was the weak one who initiated it."

"I have been going on and on about having sex with you since we first started dating. You've been strong for so long. This is one time you just wanted to please me and that's why I love you for it. I know it makes you feel bad because of your relationship with God, but as you always say, 'God is a forgiving God'. Let's pray and ask God to forgive for our sins," Desire suggested, knowing Bam didn't want to do anything to stifle his close relationship with God.

"Okay," he agreed.

"Heavenly Father, Bam and I come before you today

asking you to cleanse us in your blood and forgive us of our sins. Father God, I desire Bam sexually, but we both know sex before marriage isn't Christ-like. Thank you for helping both of us control our urges, in Jesus name, we pray, Amen."

After the prayer, it was as if the dark cloud over Bam had disappeared and the pair began making genuine small talk.

"Are you going somewhere?" Bam asked, noticing how Desire was dressed.

"Yes, I tried to tell you, but we got a little side tracked. I'm going to meet Victoria for drinks. I understand you're not fond of her, but she is my friend and has not done anything but try to help me. Just give her a chance, baby," Desire suggested.

"Maybe, I will. Besides, at this point I'm in no place to judge. Go have fun. I will be here when you get back," he said before clearing the table and placing the plates in the dishwasher.

"See you later. I will be back in a few hours." Desire kissed Bam on the cheek and headed out the door.

* * * * *

Victoria was already waiting at the bar of Bahama Breeze restaurant for Desire.

"Hey girl," Desire greeted her with a hug.

"Hi," Victoria said smiling.

"I'm so glad that we could get together. I'm sorry I was a little late. I had a time trying to get out the house," Desire began to explain.

Desire's phone began to ring. She paused her conversation long enough to take a look at caller ID. It was Bam and she sent him to voicemail. She'd just walked in, so the last thing she wanted was to interrupt their meeting with a phone call.

"Sorry about that," she said then continued her conversation. "At times, Bam doesn't want me to go anywhere."

"Men can act that way," Victoria giggled knowing the truth behind his resistance. She wasn't sure how much longer she was going to keep up with this charade. Her good friend, Desire, was involved with a rapist and was oblivious to it. Who knows if he had raped anyone else over the years. It would be hard for Victoria to forgive herself if Bam struck again on another woman.

"For some reason, he is so against us being friends."

"Umph...for some reason, huh?" Victoria said sarcastically, then rolled her eyes before taking a sip of her wine.

"Bam feels as though you have some sort of hidden agenda."

"If I was you, I'd be more concerned about his hidden agenda," Victoria spat.

"Is there something you want to tell me?" Desire asked, picking up on Victoria's ill vibe.

"Matter of fact, there is," Victoria began to say then paused.

"Okay, so what is it?"

"Nothing. Let's not talk about Bam. This is our time."

Victoria didn't have the courage to tell her at the time. Desire was convinced that Victoria was hiding something. She wouldn't dare press the issue though. Victoria was stubborn and wasn't easily persuaded.

"Welcome to Bahama Breeze, what can I get you to

drink?" the bartender asked just in time.

"Amaretto Sour with extra cherries," Desire said.

Victoria already had a glass of Riesling.

"So what's been going on? How's work?" Desire asked after ordering her drink. A change of subject was definitely necessary.

"Busy, busy and more busy. I love working labor and delivery because of the babies. I spend a lot of time in the NICU and you know I love my babies. Plus, I feel as though I'm making a difference in the maternity world. I can't complain; I really love what I do. What about you?" Victoria asked after giving her response.

"The salon is up and coming. I'm so excited about inviting you to the grand opening. It's going to be a salon and spa in one. I've been starting to interview a little more. I have to get the right people in there to fit the image I'm trying to portray. I want an upscale, chic, modern environment," Desire explained.

Two more calls came from Bam. Again, Desire sent them to voicemail. Minutes later, she received a text that read: *Call me.*

She texted back: *Is everything ok? If so, I'll call you when I leave Bahama Breeze. It's quite noisy and I don't want to interrupt our meeting.*

"Congratulations. I wish you much success," Victoria said as Desire was texting.

"Thank you so much!"

Victoria ordered another glass of wine, then the pair began talking about old times. With those two glasses of wine down, Victoria seem more relaxed. She was more like the old Victoria Desire knew from high school. Time had gotten away from them. At least an hour and a half had passed as they sat at the bar chatting, drinking and laughing.

"I need to go the ladies room," Victoria said while doing a slight pee pee dance.

"Me too! The wine is running through me," They headed to the bathroom.

Desire noticed Bam coming into the door as they were walking to the ladies room. They stopped to greet him.

"Hey, babe!" Desire said slightly intoxicated.

"Let's go. I need to talk to you," Bam whispered into Desire's ear without even acknowledging Victoria.

"Victoria, we'll talk again. I'm sorry I've got to run. I will text you about the details of the grand opening."

"You do that," she replied staring right into Bam's eyes.

Desire felt tension in the air and she noticed Victoria's nose was flared and her eyes had anger in them as though she was ready to strike. As Desire walked out with Bam, she realized both of them were acting out of character. *Had these two had a relationship before,* Desire thought as she walked to her car.

"This way," Bam grabbed Desires hand leading her to his car. "I'll drive you home. We will come back for your car in the morning. It's apparent you have a buzz and that you've been drinking."

"Fine," Desire hopped in the car.

"What's your problem?" She questioned Bam's strange behavior.

"I've been calling you all night. I told you I wasn't comfortable with you hanging out with Victoria," he explained.

"Yes, I know. And I told you that didn't make sense. I mean, do you have some personal vendetta against her or something?"

"No, I don't. I just don't want you associated with certain people," Bam spat.

"I'm sorry, but none of this makes sense. What's really going on?" Desire asked, then pulled out her phone. "Better yet, I'll just call Victoria and find out."

"Hang up the phone, Desire," Bam demanded.

Desire ignored Bam as she looked through her contact list for Victoria's number.

"Hang up the phone, Desire," Bam said again, much more aggressively than before.

"Nope!" Desire said as she listened to the phone ring.

Bam grabbed the phone from her hand and then threw it out the window.

"I said to hang it up!" he yelled.

Desire didn't say a word. She looked at him in total shock. She had no idea who this man was in front of her. She'd never seen him so angry. Desire realized that she wouldn't get any answers out of Bam at that time, but this was not over by any means!

"Smash the Homie"

Chapter 15

Isis

"Ohhhhh...oh shit! Eat this pussy baby. Right there...
yessss...that feels so good," Isis said to her boo
thang as he pushed his tongue deep inside of her hole.

She knew she was playing on dangerous grounds, but it
was something about danger and sex that turned her on. If
Vada came back to the house and saw his wife with both legs
high in the air and his homeboy's face planted deep between
them, somebody was going to end up dead. It didn't matter
to Isis though; Vada had fucked her friend, so now she was
fucking his!

"Don't stop, baby. Please don't stop. I'm almost there!"
Isis moaned in pleasure. She grabbed her boo by the head
while arching her back as if the pleasure was killing her. She
contracted her vagina around his tongue.

"Ahhhh...right there, baby," Isis screamed as he put
pressure on her spot. She gripped his bald head tight, trying
to hold his lips in place on her clit. She closed her legs on
him, squeezing the sides of his ears. He struggled to breathe,
but it was obvious Isis was on the verge of an explosive
orgasm so he kept going.

"Ah fuckkkkkk…I'm cummming!" Isis yelled at the top of her lungs.

Loyal to my friends, we break bread together,
Unbreakable bonds, rich niggas, it gets no better.

Her boo's phone began to sing. He had Vada's song, Loyalty, set as his ring tone. He lifted his head from between her legs and answered the phone without hesitation.

"Damn, you gonna answer that now?" Isis asked. She had barely finished cumming and he was already trying to get on the phone.

"Why, you don't expect me to answer it or something?" he answered her question with another question.

"It's your man, Vada," he told her.

"Oh shit! Yeah, answer that, baby!" Isis said with fear in her voice.

"Oh, you scared now, huh?" he laughed.

"Hell yeah, that nigga might be coming home right now," Isis stated.

"Yo, what up nigga?" he asked as he smirked at Isis.

"Hey, where you at?" she could hear Vada ask.

"I'm at a freak's house right now. What's up doe?" he said.

Isis just looked at him like he was stupid. She had a problem listening to him call her a freak, but deep inside she knew that's how it looked. After all, she was fucking her man's friend. She playfully swung at him attempting to hit him on the arm, but he dodged her. He retaliated by smacking her on the ass hard.

"What the fuck was that? You fucking a bitch and smacking that ass or something nigga?" Vada asked.

"Damn, Vada, what you need nigga? I'm in the middle of something," he said trying to see what Vada was calling for.

"I was trying to come through the studio," Vada said.

"Okay. I'll meet you there. I'm leaving out now," he lied, then hung up the phone.

"Your ass is wrong for calling me a freak!" Isis pouted as soon as he hung up.

"I call it like I see it, baby girl. Any chick that smashes the homie is a freak, point blank period," he said to her.

"I can't believe you talking to me like that. I thought you cared about me," Isis said with uncertainty.

"Are you serious?" he laughed while shaking his head.

"Yes, I am serious," Isis answered. "We've been kicking it, off and on, for a while now. You don't sex me like I'm a freak. You do for me. So why would I think you look at me as a freak?" Isis asked.

"Didn't I tell you that I had a wife when we first started messing around?" he asked while staring directly into her eyes.

"Yes, you told me. I'm married too. So what's you point?" she asked.

"So you should understand that me loving you is a bad idea."

"But you eat my pussy, screw me without a condom, and bust inside me whenever you want and there's nothing to it?" Isis asked with a confused look on her face.

"Exactly," he responded full of sarcasm.

Isis couldn't believe how blunt and hurtful he was being to her. Her mouth was wide open as she witnessed him demean her and get irritated by her questions.

"That's fucked up. And to think I saw some good in you because you had a wife and family. I feel for your wife. She must not be that damn bright either." Isis tried to get back at him for hurting her.

Everything immediately froze. Then it started to move again, but in slow motion. Isis could feel the rage building up inside him. Before she knew it her face had caught the backside of his hand. She didn't even have time to react. She went flying back onto the bed while holding her mouth.

"I don't want to hear nothing else about this shit!" he yelled out.

Isis didn't respond. She lay on her bed motionless, in the fetal position, holding her jaw like he had broken it. She could taste blood in her mouth and the side of her face tighten as it began to swell.

"Don't ever bring my wife up in a conversation again, bitch!" he yelled.

It was obvious Isis had hit a soft spot. She managed to get a few words out. "I'm sorry. Please don't hit me again," she pleaded.

"What you need to do is get your shit together and get your ass ready to move this package for me tonight," he said, reminding Isis of the task at hand.

Since she and Vada weren't together anymore, she'd been running packages to get a little money on the side. She had grown tired of asking Vada for money all the time. Besides, she needed to show him she didn't need his ass.

"I will get it done."

"That's a good girl. That's what I like to hear," he whispered, and then kissed her on the cheek.

DESIRE

Isis watched as he walked out the door. She began to wonder what she had gotten herself into.

"Hospital Stalker"

Chapter 16

Victoria

As Victoria was walking to the hospital entrance, she felt great. Starbucks' skinny caramel latte and a protein pack had given her a bit more energy. Not to mention, she skipped sleeping over Winston's house and had a night alone with reruns of Law and Order SVU.

"Good morning, Victoria," the hospital volunteer greeted her.

"Good morning," she smiled back.

"Hello, Victoria," another voice spoke.

It was Bam. He stood before her with a box of Baby Ruth candy bars. During her childhood and teenage years, they were her favorite candy. It had been years since she had even laid eyes on them or eaten them. The sight of the chocolate covered in peanuts made her stomach churn.

"What the hell are you doing here?" she asked in a low tone voice.

She didn't want to alarm any patients or staff members.

"I brought a peace offering. We need to talk, now," Bam said.

"No..." Victoria said, then began to walk away.

"Victoria, I'm so glad that I found you in the lobby. The patient in room one is in labor; she's dilated to eight centimeters. I think we're ready for you," a nurse explained.

Victoria looked at Bam with cold eyes and walked away to do her duty of delivering babies. On her way to the patient's room, she thought Bam had some nerve coming to her place of business. Quickly, Victoria changed into her scrubs and assisted with the delivery of the baby.

"Two more pushes and that handsome son of yours will be here," Victoria instructed.

"No, I can't do it."

"Please Ann, listen to me. Take deep breaths. You need to push to get the baby out," Victoria coached her patient.

"I'm tired and in so much pain. I can't push. I don't have the strength."

"Yes, you can."

"No, I will not..." she said before passing out.

"Prep her for surgery. We'll have to perform an emergency cesarean," Victoria instructed her team. Immediately, Victoria paged an OB/GYN. Thankfully, Dr. Rankin met her in the operating room and performed the surgery. Within thirty minutes, the baby was delivered. Victoria completed the rest of the patient's care in the surgical room. When Ann woke up, Victoria and the patient's husband were the first two people that she saw.

"Where's my son?" she asked in a weak tone.

"He's in the nursery," Victoria explained holding her hand.

"Is he all right?"

"Yes," her husband, Howard, nodded his head.

"That son of yours has an excellent grip. I fed him a

bottle."

"I'm so thankful," Ann said after taking deep breaths.

"I will return to check on you before I leave for the evening," Victoria explained before walking out the patient's room.

By now, it was lunchtime. Victoria was starving and was in the mood for soup and an apple. She headed down to the cafeteria.

"Ms. Brown, how are you feeling today?" she asked the cashier.

"I'm feeling better than usual. My son, his wife and my grandbabies are coming to visit this weekend. How are you doing, darling?"

"I'm keeping busy," she admitted.

"Sugar, you enjoy the rest of your day. It was lovely seeing you."

"Thanks and same to you."

Victoria spotted an empty table in the corner. After she dashed salt and pepper on her potato soup, Bam came and sat down next to her.

"Victoria, please. I know you're busy. I have something I need to get off my chest. All I ask is for a few moments of your time."

Without saying a word, Isis threw the sweet tea in Bam's face. Afterwards, she didn't move an inch or blink an eye. She just remained sitting, and calmly grabbed her apple and took a bite. Bam grabbed a napkin, wiped his face then left the table. Victoria shocked herself by her actions. Aggression was never part of her character, but the sight of Bam sent her into a rage.

The day was winding down as Victoria made her final rounds. Her patient, Ann, had effectively bonded with her baby and was now resting. Victoria still had three more patients to follow up with the next morning. She grabbed their charts and placed them in her office. She glanced out the window as she took off her lab coat and laid down her stethoscope. The sun was beginning to set. A few vehicles were still lingered in the parking lot. There was calm in the air. She decided to give Winston a call. She knew it was a must she saw him after work. He couldn't go two nights without her. As Victoria took a long breath, she dialed Winston's phone number on her cell phone. The phone was on the fourth ring and she hoped it would go to voicemail. She wanted to dodge Winston.

"Hey," he said, picking up before the final ring.

"Hi, Winston, how are you?"

"I'm wonderful. I'm preparing you a hot bath and placing one of those steamy love novels, you like to read, right beside the tub."

Victoria would have felt bad if she would have turned Winston down. Besides, he did give wonderful foot and neck massages.

"All right. I'm heading to the car now. I've had a long day. I don't have the energy to cook."

"That's fine. Let's just order Chinese food and have it delivered. I will see you in a few minutes, darling."

"Okay, I'm going to stop at the store for a bottle of wine. Give me twenty minutes."

"I will see you in a bit," he said.

After ending her call with Winston, Victoria grabbed her

purse and headed out the door.

"Good night!" she said to a few coworkers as she walked into the parking garage.

"That box of chocolate candy was twenty dollars. I don't like to waste money. You should be grateful that I gave you anything," Bam commented after approaching from a dark corner.

Victoria didn't respond. She totally ignored him and proceeded to get in her vehicle. Bam rushed up behind her. He grabbed her neck and pinned her against the car.

"Victoria, I have been patient with you all day. I have been at this hospital the entire day, waiting for the right opportunity to speak with you. You even threw your drink in my face. Now, you're going to listen to me. You got that?" he asked choking her even harder.

"Yes," Victoria nodded her head.

"I want to apologize for that little incident in high school. I'm asking for your forgiveness. It's been ten years and I just want to make things right."

"Incident? Are you kidding me? It wasn't an incident, Bam! You fucking raped me! You forced my clothes off and you took my virginity. You took my womanhood! You took my joy! That's not a fucking incident. You ruined my life and I hate you for that!" Victoria screamed in a rage as tears flowed down her face.

"I know. I know…and I'm sorry for that. I wish I could take it all back. In high school I didn't take no for an answer. I was young and dumb. Now, my life has changed completely. I found God and He has led me to a woman that I want to settle down with. You know it's Desire. If she, my family members, coworkers, and church family found out that I committed rape, it will ruin my livelihood. Please, I begging you, let's just put the past behind us," Bam explained, releasing the grip he had around her neck.

"Listen, I just want to go home. Please, just let me go," Victoria begged as she rummaged through her purse.

She pretended to be looking for her keys, but she was truly trying to find her stun gun. Once she located it, she continued to act as if she was truly listening and placed the stun gun behind her back. While talking, Bam constantly turned around nervously looking across the parking garage. He wanted to make sure no one popped up on him.

"So, can this be swept under the rug? You have a life and so do I," he suggested.

Victoria didn't respond. Instead she struck him with the stun gun. She hit him many times, starting with his stomach, neck, face, legs and penis repeatedly. Bam fell to the ground convulsing.

"You listen to me, motherfucker. I'm not promising you anything. You come to my job, making demands. Don't you ever come here again! Do you hear me?" Victoria asked after striking him again.

She kicked him in the face and blood went gushing everywhere.

"Stop please," he begged.

"Wow, those are the same words I said to you, ten years ago. Always remember, no deed ever goes unpunished. I don't accept your apology," Victoria said before spitting in his face.

She hopped into her vehicle and drove away, never

looking back. At the stop light, she grabbed her cell phone from her purse and dialed 911.

"911, what's your emergency?" the operator asked.

Victoria paused for a moment, "There's no emergency. I accidentally pressed the wrong button on the phone," she lied, then hung up the phone.

As Victoria sat at the stop light, she wondered if she could kill Bam and get away with it. Would doing so take away the pain and deep wounds that she'd felt for so long?

"Picking up the Pieces"

Diamond Diva
SERIES

Chapter 17

Angel

It had been several days since Angel had spoken to her friend, Isis, but this particular day she was on her mind pretty heavy. So without hesitation, Angel picked up the phone and dialed Isis's number. The phone rang several times then went to voicemail. Angel didn't leave a message. Instead she went downstairs to Sylvester's office and called Isis's home phone.

"Hello," Isis answered on the first ring.

"Wow, so that's what it takes to get in contact with you?" Angel said realizing, that the only reason Isis answered was because she didn't recognize the number.

"I guess," she mumbled.

"So, how have you been?" Angel asked.

"Fine."

"And the kids?"

"Fine I guess. They been at my momma's house."

"Oh, okay. Well, it's nice to have a break from the kids sometime. So what have you been up to?" Angel said, totally ignoring Isis's mean demeanor.

"Doing me," Isis said.

"Oh okay. Well, I haven't been doing much lately. Destiny

has been asking about her bestie, so we should do a play date soon."

"Destiny may need to find a new bestie because I don't know if there will be anymore play dates," Isis said with slurred speech.

Angel could tell Isis had been drinking. That really worried her. Isis had struggled with alcoholism in the past and Angel was concerned she'd fallen onto that path once again.

"Have you been drinking, Isis?"

"Yes, I have. And…?"

"I'm just worried because of your past," Angel said honestly.

"Listen, I'm fine. Okay? I thought I told you the last time we spoke, you need to be worried about your husband and not me."

Angel already knew Isis would probably pull that stunt again, so this time she was prepared. She didn't let it bother her one bit. Those words went in one ear and out the other. There was a more important issue to address and it was her well-being.

"Isis, this is Angel you're talking to. I am not your enemy. I have never been your enemy so you can stop with the anger."

Isis was silent, she didn't say a word, but moments later Angel heard a sniffle.

"It's okay Isis. I know you are hurt. You've always been so strong, but sometimes you have to let down the guard."

"I'm just tired Angel. I'm tired of trying to get my life to where I want it to be. I had a life and a future, but it ended when I became a teenage mother. Then I went to jail for Vada and now he's reaching his goals while I'm here stuck,"

Isis explained between tears.

"You're not stuck. It's never too late to reach for your goals. Go back to school or start that business you talked about with your old friend from jail. Work on your marriage, don't give up so easily." Angel tried speaking words of encouragement to her friend.

"That's easy for you to say. You have a whole support system set up. I don't. I don't have people behind me cheering me on and wishing the best and helping me to succeed. Haven't you realized we come from two different worlds, Angel? You will never understand my pain," Isis yelled.

The more they spoke, Angel realized she probably wasn't going to get very far with Isis. She was obviously intoxicated and not very receptive. She loved her friend, but enough was enough.

"Okay, Isis. It looks like right now isn't a good time to chat, so I'll just let you go," Angel said before hanging up the phone.

She didn't even wait for Isis to say goodbye. Being her friend was beginning to get draining. She found herself constantly giving into the relationship, but never receiving anything in return. In a final attempt to save their friendship, Angel turned to God in prayer.

"Father, God, I come before You today, with my heart heavy for my friend, Isis. She is broken and it hurts to see her in pain. Thank You for healing her body, mind and soul. Reveal Yourself to her even more so she can cling to You instead of a bottle. Rip that drinking spirit out of her, in Jesus name, Amen," Angel prayed aloud while kneeling down in Sylvester's office.

As she sat deep in meditation she heard a noise come from his laptop. She opened the laptop.

"Sexy Sagittarius has logged on," the automated voice said.

"Sylvester, where are you? Come out and play, Daddy. It's our special night. It's Sexy Sagittarius calling for you, baby," said a woman's voice from the screen.

Angel turned the lights off and contemplated clicking on the pop up box to take a look at this woman that was inviting her husband to a good time. Her heart beat accelerated. She was in disbelief that Sylvester was still doing the exact same thing they had talked about and even sought counseling over. For the first time, Angel felt that Isis might be right. She needed to be more concerned about her own marriage. Angel didn't appreciate her forgiveness being taken for weakness. Without further delay, she quickly clicked on the pop box on the laptop screen.

"There you are. I've already ran your credit card number so we're good to go for tonight," she said after kissing the screen.

Angel nodded her head. She wanted to see what these women had over her. This particular girl definitely wasn't as pretty as her. She was younger and had a bigger butt, but that was about it. Angel was always taught mental stimulation and the ability to be a wife was more important than sexual satisfaction. In this case it looks as though that wasn't so true after all.

Sexy Sagittarius did a strip tease and masturbated. After fifteen minutes into the session, Angel logged off the laptop. She snatched the laptop off the desk and headed straight for the garage where she retrieved a hammer and smashed the laptop, then went back inside and threw it into Sylvester's office.

"The Start of a War"

Diamond Diva
SERIES

Chapter 18

Isis

"Sup," Vada greeted Isis in their bedroom.

He walked in with a strange look on his face. Isis wasn't sure how to take it. He hadn't been home in over a week and the buzz she had from several glasses of wine had her judgment a little flawed. She watched as he rumbled through clothes in the closet.

Vada felt Isis stare, but didn't bother to acknowledge it. He could tell by the strong scent of alcohol and the empty wine bottles that she'd been drinking. The house didn't feel like home to him, anymore.

"So what the fuck you been up to, Isis?" Vada asked, knowing she'd been up to more than she would ever reveal to him.

Isis ignored him while she sipped on a half-empty bottle of Merlot. Her eyes were glued to the television; catching the latest episode of Basketball Wives.

"Where my kids at, yo?" Vada stood in front of the television blocking her view.

"Not here," Isis said while lying back in the bed and pulling the covers to her shoulders.

"I miss my kids. I haven't seen them in a week. That's why I came here."

"You could have taken them when you left."

"Yeah, right, as if you would have let me."

"You only miss those kids when it's convenient for you," Isis snickered in an annoying tone.

The thought of their kids tugged on her heart. Their daughter asked about her daddy on a daily basis and now the baby was saying, "Dada." Isis had just finished crying her heart out and didn't want to give Vada the satisfaction of seeing her hurt and broken down. So she put on her mad black woman face in hopes the anger would mask her pain.

"That's not true. I love my fucking little soldiers more than I love myself."

"Your daughter is not a soldier and neither is your son. I refuse to let that street mentality bullshit you live be embedded in my kid's heads. I came from a good, wholesome, working class home. Then I met your sorry ass...and look where it got me. Teenage pregnancy, getting locked up, I'm a felon and have made my life ten times harder because of the poor choices that I have made. Thank you so much Vada!" Isis yelled.

"Okay, Isis, it's my fault. That's what you want to hear?" he admitted.

"No, it's my fault. That's why I'm so angry. I should have left you a long time ago."

"Damn, Isis, I messed up. I fucked your life up. I should have never let you take the wrap and go to jail. I apologize."

"Over and over again, you have messed up. Now, you can shut up. I'm tired of hearing the same thing. Not only did you fuck me, but your fucked my friend. Desire was one of the few dear friends I had and you went and fucked her!" Isis got up in Vada's face.

"I didn't know she was your friend. I didn't have a malicious hidden agenda of fucking your friend who I barely knew existed in your life. I haven't attempted to contact her. I saw her at the store three days ago, she told me to never contact her again because she was so distraught over what happened. I don't want her and she doesn't want me. I swear on my kids," he said, holding his hands up and inching closer to her.

"I don't accept your apology," Isis mumbled and rolled her eyes.

Vada stared at his wife. He could see the hurt in her face.

"Wait a minute, what happened to your face?" he asked after noticing what looked like old bruising. Vada turned on the lights and the lamp next to the bed so that he could get a better look. "Isis, what happened to your face?" he asked again.

"You don't get to ask me any more questions," Isis tried avoiding the question.

"Aah, all right, I get it. Now shit is coming together," Vada said, realizing the rumors he'd heard were possibly true.

"What's coming together, Vada?"

"Word on the street is you fucking with the homie," he responded, and pulled the cell phone out of his jean pocket.

"You fucked my friend so what if I did smash the homie?" Isis spat.

Vada hadn't heard Isis was fucking with his boy, but he

did hear she was running packages for him. But from the way Isis was talking, she was fucking him too. Vada's heart began to race. He didn't know if he wanted to bruise up the other side of Isis's face or bust a cap in his homie's ass.

"I'm coming for you, boy," Vada said into the cell phone then hung up.

Vada ran out of the house without even finishing his conversation with Isis. Everything in Isis told her to stop Vada from leaving the house, but she didn't have the energy to run after him.

Isis warmed up some old chicken wings she'd brought home form the club and finished her bottle of wine. An hour later, she decided to lie down. Her cell phone had been ringing repeatedly since Vada had left. She figured it was him calling, so she didn't even bother looking until now.

"Hello," she yelled into the cell phone.

"Before you hang up, I want you to know how truly sorry I am for sleeping with Vada. I didn't know he was your husband. If I would have known, I would have kept it moving." It was Desire and she was attempting to apologize.

"You were my friend, Desire. I trusted you and you slept with my husband! I just can't get over the betrayal."

"I want to still have a friendship. You are one of the few friends I have. Every day I think about you and ways of repairing our friendship."

"I don't know if that's possible," Isis honestly said.

"I will do whatever it takes to get your friendship back. I've even started the salon and spa we talked about in jail and I want you to part of it. This was OUR dream, not just mine."

"Desire, you have to give me some time. Please," Isis said then hung up the phone.

Once again she found herself crying uncontrollably. It seemed as though her days had turned into constant cycles of fighting, arguing, crying and drinking.

"Indecent Proposal"

Diamond Diva
SERIES

Chapter 19

Desire

"So you want to tell me what the other night was about?" Desire asked Bam as they were taking a light stroll around the neighborhood.

The events of the other night at the restaurant with Victoria were still haunting Desire. Until this moment, she hadn't found the right time or had the courage to ask Bam about it.

"What night, baby?" he asked with a confused look.

Desire didn't respond. She stopped in her tracks, folded her arms and looked at him like he had lost his mind.

"What? What are you talking about?" Bam inquired.

Realizing he wasn't going to willing engage in the conversation, Desire spelled it out for him. "Everything...oral sex, the negative talk about Victoria, and the scene you made at the restaurant. Not to mention you tossing my phone out the window. All of this was totally out of character for you."

"It's no big deal, baby," Bam turned to Desire and gave her a small kiss on the check. "I just don't care for Victoria. Our spirits don't agree. I want you to be careful around her; that's all."

"I'm sorry Bam, but I'm not convinced. I'm not sure that I believe you. Did something happen between the two of you?" Desire began to probe a bit.

"What are you getting at, Desire?"

"I'm just saying, I know you all attended the same high school. So maybe you guys had a secret crush or were high school sweethearts or something."

"Ha,ha,ha,ha!" Bam bent over and held his stomach as he laughed aloud. "Nooooo! I didn't do a thing with her. We weren't together in high school. Desire, I love you," he said, pulling her in close to him as he proceeded to get down on the street pavement on one knee.

"What are you doing?" Desire said in total shock as she watched Bam kneel before her.

"Shhhh," he held his index finger to his lip as an indication for her to be quiet. Then he proceeded, "Desire, you're the one for me. I'm not a man of many words, so I will keep it sweet and simple. Please know you hold the key to my heart. I want you in my life forever. I can't picture life without you. Desire, will you marry me?" he asked while placing the three carat, princess cut diamond on her finger.

"Yes! Yes!" Desire yelled with tears in her eyes.

Like a little girl, she jumped up and down in joy. Desire was totally surprised that Bam popped the question. She went straight into bride mode. The entire walk home, all she could do was talk about wedding plans. While admiring her ring, she chatted away about the colors, the location, the people she would invite and even where they should have their honeymoon. Bam just smiled and listened not wanting to interrupt her moment.

* * * * *

The next day at the spa and salon, Desire couldn't help but smile. No matter what happened she kept a smile on her face.

"Well, someone is in a pretty good mood today," one of her stylist said, noticing her permanent smile.

"Yes, I am! In fact, I'm so happy that I think we will give twenty percent off all services and products for the entire day!" she said to everyone in the shop.

"That's a kind gesture," a client said as she was checking out. "What's the occasion?"

"I'm celebrating my engagement," she said while holding up her ring in the air.

"Oh my God, congratulations!" Everyone said while giving her hugs and praises.

Desire was on cloud nine and never wanted this feeling to end. She sat in her office at the spa surfing the internet for dresses. She'd already set the wedding date for two weeks away and she'd secured a location. She was sure she wanted Isis as her matron of honor and Victoria as her maid of honor so she decided to give them a call. There wasn't much time, so she began with Victoria. After several rings her phone went to voicemail. Desire didn't bother leaving a message; this was news she wanted to deliver in person. Next she tried giving Isis a call.

"Hello?" Isis answered on the first ring.

"Helloooooo, girlie!" Desire sang into the phone.

"Well, hello. Don't you sound happy," Isis said noticing the excitement in Desire's voice.

"Yes, I am very, very, happy. In fact I haven't been this happy since they released me from jail!" They both laughed.

"I know you said you needed some time before you could jump right back into our friendship, but we've had a few conversations since then and I think we're progressing," Desire stated.

"Yeah. I can't lie, we have made quite a bit of progress."

"Well, I want to invite you to lunch so we can chat. I have some exciting things happening in my life and I want you to part of it," Desire explained.

"Okay, that's cool, as long as you choose a spot that serves alcohol."

"Will do. I'll call you tomorrow and we can decide on a place and time."

"Okay," Isis agreed before hanging up.

After speaking with Isis, Desire headed out to the salon to monitor the floor. As she passed a customer, she noticed she had dropped her credit card. Desire picked up the credit card from the floor and felt a wave of nausea come over her. The room started to spin. She felt hot and cold all at the same time. She gathered herself long enough to speak to the client.

"All right, Ms. Harper, we'll see you in two weeks," she concluded.

The season was changing from summer to fall and it was the beginning of flu season. With no health insurance to pay for an outrageous medical bill, the last thing Desire needed was to come down with a cold. She made a mental note to stop by the pharmacy to pick some Airborne on the way home. Desire had a business to protect. She was determined to have the doors open six days a week and she needed to be there. The weekdays were a bit slow, but the weekends were always busy. She had clients scheduled as early as 6:00 a.m.

"Is there room for one more pedicure before you close the business for the evening?" Victoria asked as she walked through the door.

"Of course. Anything for you!" Desire said directing Victoria to the pedicure station. "What are you doing here? I called you earlier, but when you didn't answer, I figured you would be at the hospital delivering babies. It's a full moon tonight," Desire laughed, referring to the old wives tale that full term ladies go into labor when there's a full moon.

"Actually, I just got off and have been on my feet all day. So I figured supporting your business would be great and we could catch up."

"Have a seat here. Can I get you some champagne, wine, water or anything?"

"Yes, wine would be nice," she nodded her head.

Victoria was impressed with the modern décor of the salon mixed with elegance. Light Jazz music lingered in the air. It had a relaxing feeling. All the staff wore all black and presented themselves in the most respectable manner. In the corner sat a small refreshment area stocked with an assortment of beverages, snacks and finger foods. This was an environment Victoria was accustomed to and she wouldn't mind getting her pampering done here.

Desire quickly prepared wine and cheese for Victoria then returned to the nail technician.

"Victoria, let me apologize for the other night," She said as she handed Victoria the refreshments.

"Apologize for what?"

"My behavior. I think I drank a bit too much. Plus, I'm sorry for Bam's behavior. He was very cold towards you. He doesn't trust easily and is very protective over me."

"I'm glad you mentioned that night at the restaurant, I wanted to speak with you about that night."

"I'm all ears," Desire pulled up a seat next to Victoria."

"Well Bam..." Victoria began to say.

"Yes. Go on," Desire said eager to hear what Victoria had to say.

"Well, I just wanted to say that you and Bam seem to be getting closer," Victoria said instead of telling her the ultimate truth that he's been hiding.

"We are. I believe he is my soul mate," Desire proclaimed.

"Don't rush into anything. You haven't even been with him a year yet. You should be in cautious mode," Victoria attempted to drop a subtle hint.

"I'm not rushing. I just know in my heart that he's the one for me. I love him so much. Don't you feel that way about Winston?" Desire inquired, hoping Victoria would share her feelings.

"I grew to love Winston over time," Victoria lied. She didn't love Winston; never had, never did, and probably never will. Victoria's heart was not open and far too broken to truly let anyone in.

"What color do you want on your toes?" the technician interrupted their conversation.

"A soft peach," Victoria said as the nail technician rubbed her feet.

Desire smiled as she watched her friend finish up her

pedicure. She wondered what was truly going on with Victoria. She'd known her for a long time and something just didn't seem right. She didn't know if Victoria was hiding something or if she was just simply unhappy, but she was determined to get to the bottom of things. For now, the big engagement announcement would have to wait.

"Walls Closing In"

Chapter 20

Angel

Angel wasn't ready to confront Sylvester about the latest event. For the past week he had been out of town for a pastor's conference. When he would call to check on her and Destiny, Angel acted as if everything was just fine. She didn't want to give any inclination there was a problem. This particular night, Sylvester was at a treasury meeting at the church with some of the trustees. While he was there, Angel pondered on how to proceed with their marriage. She hadn't quite decided how she was going to handle Sylvester's porn addiction and constant lies, but she wanted to explore all of her options.

The first option was divorce. She wrote down the pros and cons of getting a divorce. She considered all the things she would expect if she chose to go that route. Of course she wanted full custody of Destiny, alimony and the house. Angel was seriously contemplating getting legal advice from an attorney. If she didn't proceed with the divorce she wanted to consider separation.

Angel knew she couldn't just let Sylvester continue to behave this way, nor could she accept it. She had to think

Diamond Diva
❤❤ S E R I E S ❤❤

about her daughter and what example she would be setting for her. Angel didn't fear being alone; instead, she feared longing for a man who lied about who he really was.

For the past month, Angel had been going to the bank and taking out four hundred dollars a week in cash and making a deposit into another bank account. This particular day, she was going to take out an extra five hundred dollars. Sylvester let her control the joint bank account—as long as the bills were paid, he didn't care. Angel knew Sylvester probably had a private bank account for himself as well. She was tired of him spending their money, which was ultimately the Lord's money, on porn and whores.

Sylvester knew the board members suspected something fishy as he walked into the financial meeting that had already begun without him. Four meetings had been held prior to this one in an attempt to discover where ten thousand dollars from the church had gone. Sylvester knew exactly where it had gone, but he also knew the wire transfer he sent to Desire was untraceable. Therefore, he was not the least bit worried about them finding out. Sylvester considered himself much smarter than most of the members on the board.

"Hello, Bishop. Glad you could join us," one of the Deacons said pulling out a chair for Sylvester to have a seat.

"Hello. Sorry I'm a little late," he said as he was seated.

"We would like to get right to the point if you don't mind," the deacon said while standing.

"Okay," Sylvester nodded.

"Bishop, we know about the addiction you're struggling with. We also know the missing money is somehow connected to your personal financial debt," the deacon said while looking Sylvester directly in the face.

Sylvester was taken off guard by this statement. He couldn't believe what he was hearing. He wasn't sure how to react. His mind raced with all sorts of questions, *Should I deny it? Where did they get their information? Did Angel come to one of the ministers about or marital problems?* He could feel beads of sweat developing on his head and his palms got sweaty. He swallowed in an attempt to get rid of the lump that was forming in his throat.

"It's okay. We don't expect you to respond. In fact, we really aren't interested in your excuse," the deacon said before sitting down.

Another deacon stood up, "Please contact this counselor," he handed Sylvester a pamphlet then continued. "Because the reputation of the entire church is at stake, we will keep this little situation a secret and will not reveal it to anyone outside of this room. It's mandatory that you get help."

At that point everyone in the room stood up and walked out. That was Sylvester's indication the meeting was adjourned and the board was not happy. When the last person left and closed the door behind them, Sylvester let out a huge sigh of relief. He glanced over the pamphlet the deacon handed him, and then he picked up the phone to contact his bank. The deacons were right, he had accumulated quite a bit of personal debt and he was in the process of trying to refinance his house. His spending on cybersex and high-end prostitution had gotten out of control. He thought back to just a couple weeks ago at the couples' retreat when he spent a thousand dollars on a prostitute. In the middle of the night, when his wife was fast asleep he snuck off to a nearby room. He'd arranged for one of his regular girls to come to the resort for an hour a fun. Now he was regretting that decision. All of his credit cards were maxed out, and if he dipped into their joint account, he knew Angel would start getting suspicious. Sylvester felt ashamed as he waited for the banker to come on the line to discuss the status of his refinance application.

"Hey, old man!" Bam opened the door to Sylvester's office and let himself in.

"What's up, youngster?" Sylvester quickly hung up the phone.

"How's the family?"

"Angel and Destiny are doing well. How are you?" Sylvester inquired.

"You know, I can't complain. I'm actually in a pretty good place in my life right now," Bam said with a glow.

"Wow! I know that look. Somebody has found love." Sylvester said noticing the twinkle in Bam's eye that he, himself had when he found his true love, Angel.

"You sure you're not a prophet?" Bam laughed. "As a matter of fact, I have found that special someone and I asked her to marry me," he proudly said.

"Is that so? Who is this lucky lady?"

"It's Desire; you met her briefly at the couples' retreat."

"Oh, yeah," Sylvester almost choked on his words. "Congrats," he managed to say then began to cough. A knot formed in his stomach and those same sweaty palms and beads of sweat from early reappeared. He tried to prepare himself because he knew what was going to be said next.

"I would like for you to marry us," Bam asked exactly

what Sylvester predicted.

"Of course, I will. I'm really happy for the two of you," he lied.

"Thank you. I have got to run and get back to work. We're doing this pretty quick; the date is set for two weeks from now. I'll have her get you the specifics," Bam said smiling before heading out the office.

Sylvester didn't even bother calling the bank back. Instead he cleared off his desk and headed home. He had a slight headache and wanted to just go home and get some rest. Once he reached his car, Sylvester turned on some soothing music and began to drive. The entire ride he thought of all the things he's done and how it has negatively impacted his life. He was in jeopardy of losing all his assets due to debt, along with his marriage and church due to infidelity. Not to mention, Bam was about to marry a woman he'd had sex with.

Sylvester was a nervous wreck as he drove down 85 North. He felt the walls were caving in on him and at a rapid pace. Those sweat beads and sweaty palms from early had reappeared again. His heart was pounding to the point that his chest began to hurt and he felt as though he couldn't breathe.

"Oh, my God! I'm having a heart attack!" Sylvester said aloud.

In a panic, he began to pray silently as he tried to pace his breathing by taking a few deep breaths. His eyesight was blurred, but when he looked ahead he could see a hospital sign. Without hesitation, Sylvester decided to drive straight there. He pulled directly in front of the emergency room entrance and walked right in. By this time his shirt was drenched in sweat.

"Please! I need to see a doctor. I'm having a heart attack!" he yelled as soon as he walked in.

Moments later, a nurse arrived with a wheelchair and quickly took him off to the back. After a full work up, it was determined he'd experienced a panic attack.

"Honey! Are you okay?" Angel walked in with the doctor.

"He's just fine," the doctor responded to Angel, then directed his attention to Sylvester. "You're the leader of a large church which can be quite stressful. What you experienced was a panic attack. It has many similar symptoms as a heart attack, but it's not nearly as serious. I'm glad you came in as a precaution," the Emergency Department doctor informed him.

"Oh, thank God," Angel sang out and Sylvester nodded his head in agreement.

"In the meantime, I'm going to give you a medication called Xanax. It will relieve anxiety and help you to relax. Be sure to only take these pills as directed," the doctor instructed.

"Will do, thank you for your time, doc." Sylvester hopped off of the small, uncomfortable hospital bed and grabbed his clothes.

Angel assisted him getting dressed. They moved his car to the visitor's parking lot after deciding Sylvester shouldn't drive. The ride home was quiet. Sylvester attempted making small talk, but it was apparent Angel was being distant. He even went as far as to mention Bam's engagement, but not even that got a response from her. They both sat in silence the rest of the ride home as the music played in the background.

"Just Say No"

Chapter 21

Victoria

"So what was it that you wanted to talk to me about?" Victoria asked Winston hoping he wasn't proposing on this very night, or at all for that matter.

"Well, Victoria, you and I have been together for quite a while."

"Yes," she said with her stomach cringing.

"So I can confide in you about anything."

"Of course," Victoria agreed.

"My buddy, Dexter, you remember him, right?"

"I do remember him."

"His girlfriend cheated on him. Well, it's been a year since it has happened. The dust has settled. She claims she cheated because she had "Daddy" issues. Her father did the same thing so she repeated the pattern. Now, she wants to get back with him," Winston explained.

"Does he want the same?"

"Yes, he still loves her; but, of course, he's scared. I'm not sure what to tell him."

"Does he think about her every day?"

"Yes, several times a day. I have grown tired of him

speaking of her. Being the good friend I am, I just listen."

"If he thinks of her that much, he should consider forgiving her and if he decides to work things out with her, there should be boundaries set. Both need to be accountable for their actions." Vitoria explained with confidence as though she was a licensed couples' therapist of some sort.

"You're right, thanks, babe," Winston replied before biting his chicken piccata entrée.

Victoria and Winston were enjoying a five-course meal at the exclusive restaurant called Dolci. It took two weeks just to get a reservation for a decent table. Winston knew Victoria enjoyed the finer things in life and he took pride in giving her just that at every opportunity.

Victoria's cell phone rang. Her first bite of mouthwatering manicotti would have to wait just in case it was the hospital calling.

"Hello," she answered the unfamiliar number.

"Hey, chica," she recognized Desire's voice right away.

"Hey, hun. How are you?"

"Wonderful! I have some great news to spill to you," Desire said full of excitement.

"Really? What's the good news?" Victoria inquired.

"Bam proposed to me!" she yelled into the phone.

"Wow! Someone's getting married, huh?" Winston interjected, hearing Desire screams through the phone.

There was an awkward pause.

"Victoria, are you still on the line?" Desire asked in response to the silence.

"Yes, I am. It's bad reception where I am. Congratulations sweetie."

"Well, the wedding date is set for two weeks. I know its short notice, but I would love to have you as my maid of honor."

"Oh...really? Give me second. I'm going to check my calendar on my phone."

"All right."

Victoria pretended to look at her phone calendar then returned. "Desire, unfortunately, I'm going to be out of state for the next few weeks at a conference. You know I will send a gift and to make up for my absence. I will definitely be at your bridal shower."

"Oh, okay, I totally understand. It's such short notice."

"Listen, I have to run, but I will call you later on in the week. I will help you in any way that I can to plan the ceremony." Victoria ended the conversation in the most polite way possible.

"Thanks, Victoria. It means a lot to me to have your support."

"So who's getting married?" Winston asked.

"Desire and Bam."

"How nice. What's with the long face? You don't look so happy," Winston said noticing disapproval on Victoria's face.

"I think she may be rushing into something. She isn't pregnant, so there's no need for the shotgun wedding."

"I thought you valued marriage," Winston said with a confused look on his face.

"Yes, I do when it's the right time and with the right person. On a lighter note, how's your entrée?" Victoria asked caressing Winston's hand. She was a master at diversion.

"Scrumptious."

As Winston and she ate their dinner, Victoria wondered how she could get the courage to warn Desire about Bam prior to the wedding date.

"Deadly Ending"

Diamond Diva
♦♦SERIES♦♦

Chapter 22

Isis

I sis hadn't seen her children in seven days. Unless, it was lifting her finger to light up and smoke a cigarette and having a bottle put to her lips, she didn't have the energy for it. Her oldest one was starting to go through the asking "why" phase. Isis knew she couldn't handle her daughter asking her where Daddy was and why he wasn't home. Vada had only called in the wee hours of the morning two days ago. Isis thought about starting over somewhere else with no children and husband. Deep down, she loved her children; however, they were products of a failed life that she tried desperately to hold on to. Isis never really wanted children so early in life. Vada wanted children so that he could have someone to pass his last name on to. All Isis ever really wanted was a simple life without the streets, hustle, drug and the music world.

She and Desire had been talking regularly and things were almost back to where they'd left off. She forgave Desire, but deep inside she could never forget. When she received the call from Desire confirming the place and time for their lunch, Isis asked Desire to pick her up. She had been cooped up in the house for the last few days and desperately

needed to get out. She figured getting some fresh autumn air would be good for her. Isis jumped into a hot shower, then glanced in her closet. Clothes weren't an issue for her. Not only did Vada keep her closet stacked, but she could make a sweatshirt look designer and fashionable. A t-shirt, jeans and her hair in a messy bun suited her just fine.

Ding Dong! The doorbell rang. Isis grabbed her Chanel bag and headed to the front door.

"Hey, bitch, I'm starving. You're paying, I have no money," she said opening her front door.

"Hello to you, too, hooch!" Desire smiled. "Yes, the tab will be on me. You're going to be at a two drink maximum," Desire said giggling.

"Let's compromise on a four drink maximum," Isis said knowing she needed way more than two drinks to get her buzz on.

"Okay," she agreed while they both hopped into the car.

Desire decided to take Isis to Off the Sea, an upscale restaurant that served Mediterranean food.

"Welcome to Off the Sea, I'm Emily, what drinks can I get you ladies started with?" the waitress asked.

"I'll have water with lemon," Desire requested.

"And I'll have a bottle of any kind of red wine you have. I'm ready to order my entree," Isis stated. She hadn't had a decent meal in days and she was starving.

"What can I get you?" Emily asked.

"I will have the seafood medley."

"Very well then, and for you, ma`am?" the waitress asked Desire.

"I will have the same and for an appetizer we will have

the Greek sampler with extra feta cheese and olives."

"I will place your orders and will be right back with your drinks."

"Thank you," Isis said taking a deep breath.

"So how are you really feeling?" Desire asked.

She still felt remorse about the string of events that went down with Vada the night of his show and at the retreat.

"I'm making it. I haven't spoken to Vada in days. Honestly, I don't care to speak to him." Isis stated figuring that was really what Desire wanted to know.

"How are the kids?"

"They are still with my mother until I sort out my life. I don't have a next move," Isis said honestly.

She had no idea how to pick up the pieces and move forward. She'd always depended on Vada for everything. She had no real skills or education, so getting a good job was out of the question. She also had no real money. All she knew was the drug game and she really didn't want to depend on that to raise her kids.

"Well, take your time. Isis, you're just down right now. You'll know when you're ready to get back up. Besides, I could use some help in the salon," Desire gave Isis an inviting smile.

Isis didn't respond. After all, the spa and salon was originally her idea. How dare Desire ask her to help out at the salon? If she was offering a partnership then they could chat, but Isis was in no way interested in being Desire's helper.

The drinks and appetizers came just in time. Isis had not eaten a hardy meal in days and couldn't wait to dig in. The sampler tasted like a gourmet meal to her.

An hour later, the drinks had begun to creep up on Isis and the conversation became more light-hearted. The pair began talking about their time in prison together and funny encounters.

"I know you're so excited about the salon. I have to ask, how did you get the financing for it?" Isis asked. That was the million-dollar question.

"Girl you know I'm a hustler. I can get a man to buy me a castle if I try hard enough," Desire bragged.

"Bitch please. This me you talking to," Isis said then sipped from her glass of wine.

"Seriously. I hustled the money up using men," Desire declared.

"Hustled how?" Isis asked knowing it was more to the story then Desire was sharing.

"Okay let me just give you the story. When I came home I tried doing things the legit way like we'd talked about in jail, but I couldn't get any small business loans or investors anywhere. I was so determined to make our dream work that I started doing online pornography using a webcam," Desire explained.

Isis finally was getting to the truth. And when she heard the words pornography and webcam, a red flag was raised. She continued to ask questions about the webcam.

"So you made enough money off of doing internet porn to finance the entire business?"

"Well, I had sort of a celebrity clientele," Desire said.

"Oh yeah? Like who?" Isis was not letting her off so easy.

"If I tell you, will you pinky promise not to tell anyone?"

Desire made her promise.

"Sure," she answered without even a thought.

"Bishop Sylvester."

"What? Girl, shut up!" Isis yelled, nearly choking on her wine.

"He was one of my main customers. He gave me hush money not to tell anyone about his addiction to porn. I even gave him head in the church office one Sunday."

"Girl, you going to hell! That's straight to hell. Like you will not pass go or collect $200!" Isis said, then busted out laughing. "I don't believe you."

"Yes, I did. As God is my witness," Desire replied laughing holding up her right hand.

"That's crazy, Sylvester is a wild boy." Isis shook her head.

"Please keep this between the two of us. I don't want to hurt Angel."

"I won't say anything. This kind of pain is real and most of all, I don't wish it on Angel. Besides, she knows anyway. She just acts as if his sick behavior doesn't exist. If Angel doesn't wise up, she will get what she deserves."

"So she knows?"

"Of course. Listen, it's no secret Sylvester has his issues with porn. The rumors have been going on for months. Angel has even had evidence in her face. She refuses to accept the truth. She just uses God and prayer as an excuse for everything," Isis tried explaining.

The two continued to chat and Isis continued to drink. After two hours it was about time to start wrapping things up.

"I've been meaning to ask you something," Desire said

as Isis took her final sip from her wine glass.

"Oh, lawd! What's that?" Isis asked hoping Desire didn't say no crazy shit.

"Well, first let me start by saying, I'm getting married!" she smiled from ear to ear while holding up her ring.

"Oh, wow!" Isis grabbed her hand and pulled it close to her face as to examine it like a jeweler. "That's nice!" she complimented her ring.

"Thank you. But there's more."

"Okay," Isis wondered what else Desire had to say.

"I would like for you to be my matron of honor for my wedding."

"What the hell, we're cool now. I will be honored to do it," Isis said with a drunken slur.

Isis's phone had rung several times during their conversation. She shuffled through her purse and pulled it out. It was Vada.

"Hello?" she answered the phone full of attitude.

"Baby," a muffled voice said.

"Hello?" Isis yelled into the phone. She could barely hear him.

"I'm sorry," there was a pause then a deep breath. "I love you."

"Where are you?" Isis asked. She could barely hear or understand what Vada was saying.

There was no response.

"Hello? Vada?" she screamed into the phone. Something in her gut was telling her something was wrong.

"Is everything okay?" Desire asked?

"No. It's Vada. Something is wrong."

Isis's phone rang again. This time it was one of her homegirls. Although she wasn't in the mood for chatting something told her to answer.

"Hello?"

"Isis! Vada has been shot! You gotta get to the barbershop now!" the girl yelled into the phone.

"Take me to the barbershop on Sugarcreek! Vada has been shot!" Isis screamed hysterically.

Desire threw a $100 bill on the table and they both ran out the restaurant and hopped in the car. Isis was shaking in the car. For the entire car ride she was praying that God would let Vada be okay. But as they approached the barbershop, there was a yellow tape surrounding his car. Isis jumped out of Desire's car even before she was able to come to a complete stop. As she got closer to the scene she could see Vada hunched over in the driver's seat with blood all over his chest. It was apparent he was dead.

"Nooooooo!'" she screamed as she ran towards the crime scene.

The police immediately rushed her and held her back. Isis fell to her knees. She didn't have the energy to fight back.

"That's my husband. Please get off of me! Let me get to my husband!" she begged.

Desire grabbed Isis tight and held her in her arms.

"No, no, no!" Isis screamed as Desire held her like a baby, rocking her back and forth.

"Enough is Enough"

Chapter 23

Angel

Angel finally got the strength to speak with Sylvester about his porn addiction. She had little tolerance at this point and basically, she'd decided it was time they separate. After an hour-long conversation, she finally knew the truth about the money, porn and even prostitution. If it wasn't for the strength and confidence she'd received from the good Lord, she would have walked away a hurt and destroyed woman. Instead she handed it all over to Him and continued to walk with her head up high.

She left Sylvester in his office sulking like a big baby. She had no remorse and didn't even look back when she walked out. She headed upstairs to the kitchen. She had more important issues to handle. She was baking Destiny a cake and it needed to be done before she got home from school. Her little one was doing so well in school. Upon arriving home, Angel wanted to surprise her with milk in her favorite Hello Kitty cup and a slice of yellow cake with chocolate icing.

Knock, knock, knock! There was a knock on the front door. She flipped the television monitor to the outside cameras

and saw it was Bam.

"It's open," Angel said before licking the chocolate icing from her finger.

"How's it going, Miss First Lady?" Bam greeted Angel with a playful hug after he opened the door.

"I just finished baking a cake from scratch and frosting it."

"I can see that," Bam said while rummaging through the cabinet for a plate.

"May I get a slice, please?" He stood there with a plate in his hand like a five year old.

"Not until my little princess gets home from school. I made this cake especially for her," Angel explained while turning on the faucet to wash dishes.

"Okay, I'll wait. Can't upset the princess," he smiled then continued. "How's Sylvester doing?"

"Sylvester is fine. He's in his office in the basement. Now I have a question for you, mister."

"Shoot," Bam said before opening the refrigerator door and grabbing a bottle of water.

"What's this chatter I hear about you getting married?" Angel froze in motion and looked Bam in the face.

"That's actually why I'm here. I wanted to tell you in person," Bam said then took a sip of water.

"So who is this lucky lady?"

"Her name is Desire. You may remember her from the retreat."

"Yes, I do. I remember there was some sort of disturbance surrounding her." Angel said, not really knowing all the details about the situation.

"Yes, but let's not dwell on that. She's a beautiful woman and she has lots of great qualities. We vibe together and I feel like she's my soul mate," Bam pled his case.

"Okay, so why hasn't she been formally introduced to the family and our parents as of yet?" Angel quizzed Bam. "There is a proper way of handling an engagement, you know."

"I promise to cover all the bases. It's just that things happened so quickly."

"Have you guys set a date?"

"Yes, in two weeks."

"What? From the way things went at the weekend retreat, it was revealed to everyone that she slept with another man. Are you sure that you two need to be rushing into anything?" Angel questioned Bam's judgment.

Angel wasn't the type to judge people and she didn't know all the details from the retreat, but she wanted to make sure Bam didn't make any wrong decisions. After all, she had been married for years and now she's wondering if she'd made the wrong choice.

"God forgives and expects us too. You should know that better than anyone. How many times have you forgiven Sylvester for his indiscretions, or looked the other way and totally ignored it? I've heard lots of rumors about him, but who am I to judge? I love Desire very much. I love her as a person. We pray together and put God first in all we do. I'm happy. It's been a long time since I could say that."

"Look, I wasn't trying to come off as if I was questioning your love for her. If you're cool with it and dealing with the fact that she slept with another woman's man, then I will butt out." Angel threw her hands in the air.

"Angel, I'm sorry. I didn't mean to snap off at you like that. I've been putting in long hours at work and I've just been tired a lot lately. When I get home and see Desire, all those frustrations go out of the window. I just want everyone to support my decision in marriage."

"Keep seeking God about every aspect of your life. I would like to formally be introduced to her before the wedding," Angel requested while drying the dishes.

"I'll make that happen," he replied.

"Wedding Day Jitters"

Chapter 24

Desire

"I made it to the finish line," Desire said as she was admiring her Vera Wang dress that hung in front of her.

The dress was purchased from an online consignment shop and was discounted sixty percent of the original price. When she purchased it, it fit perfectly and only needed to be dry cleaned.

"Barely," Isis commented before sipping on a second glass of champagne.

"Aren't you supposed to be helping me? You are the matron of honor," Desire asked as she took the dress off the hanger and began to put it on.

"I guess. I don't see anyone else in line to help you," Isis giggled.

"I'm here to help," Angel said holding Desire's hand.

Desire shook her head and rolled her eyes in disgust of Isis's behavior. She knew she was still hurt over what happened with Vada, but drinking her life away was not the resolution.

"Thanks Angel. I'm so glad you were able to step in and take the place of my maid of honor. I don't have a maid

of honor, but now I do have two matrons, so I am truly blessed."

Desperately, Desire wanted Victoria to be the maid of honor. But with the obligations of her job, such a short notice was not feasible for her. Victoria had to decline the offer. Besides, these three women, Desire didn't have many friends. Her father was a no show to the wedding, but her mother was sitting in the front row proud of her only daughter changing her life around for the better.

"What's going on?" Desire said as she struggled to get the dress on properly.

"I can't get the fasteners to close," Angel said.

"Girl, you better suck and tuck!" Isis said as she sat and watched them struggle.

"I have an idea!" Angel said before reaching in her bag. "Try this!" She pulled out a Spanx.

"Perfect! You're a life saver!" Desire said knowing that she'd gained a bit of weight in the past few weeks.

"I originally bought it for myself but the dress fit perfectly without it. So now it's yours to keep," Angel smiled.

"Well, I got something for you too!" Isis stopped Desire as she headed to the bathroom to put on the Spanx.

"Okay, thanks," Desire grabbed the bag from Isis hand without even looking inside it.

When Desire reached the bathroom she peeped in the bag from Isis. It was a pregnancy test. She looked in the mirror at her belly that seemed to be a bit more round and hard. She figured *what the hell. I may as well put the test to use.* So she peed on the stick, laid it on the counter, and then proceeded to pull on the extra tight Spanx. Once she had it on, she walked back in the dressing room to give the wedding dress another shot.

"Why don't we have a toast? Angel suggested as soon as she walked in.

"Yes, we shall have a toast," Isis said, happy someone besides herself mentioned the bubbly.

"To Desire and Bam...may you two love each other and have a blessed and prosperous marriage," Angel said.

"Yes, same thing as she just said. Let's drink," Isis replied before gulping down a glass of champagne and then wandering off to the rest room.

Angel assisted Desire into her dress. This time it went on with ease.

"You're a life saver!" Desire hugged Angel, thankful for the Spanx.

"Spanx work wonders!"

"Oh ladies!" Isis announced as she walked back into the dressing room. "We have another reason to toast!" She sang while swirling Desires pregnancy test in the air.

"What is it now, Isis?" Desire asked not even noticing the pregnancy test in her hand.

"You're pregnant!" she said then threw back another glass of champagne.

A little bit of champagne had dribbled down her dress. Fortunately, Angel rushed over with a cloth and began to gently wipe out the light stain the drops had caused. Desire rushed over and took the test from her hand.

"Oh my God!" she said staring at the positive test.

Desire felt a little sick to her stomach as the realization of what she just discovered began to set in. She was pregnant, but she'd never had sex with Bam, her soon to be husband.

She knew she was caring Vada, her best friend's dead husband's baby. Not only that, she was finding out minutes before she was about to walk down the aisle.

"Congrats!" Angel said after getting the champagne off of Isis's dress.

"Thanks. But later for that, let's get this wedding started," Desire headed out the dressing room and towards the church sanctuary.

Desire's mother was waiting in the foyer for her and she decided it was only right for her to walk her down the aisle. Desire's mother was everything to her. The church doors opened and the small gathering of people stood up to get a glimpse of Desire. All eyes were on her, especially Bam's. Her eyes filled with tears as she walked down the aisle to meet her future husband.

"We are gathered here today in the eyes of God to join this man and woman in holy matrimony," Sylvester said after the music stopped.

Desire took a sigh of relief, grateful that the wedding ceremony turned out so nice. She knew Bam was going to make her happy and provide the life that she deserved and always dreamed of. The ceremony continued, and Desire grew anxious as she went through the usual wedding ceremony motions. All she wanted to hear was Sylvester say, "You may kiss your bride."

"Does anyone object to this marriage?" Desire's heart stopped as she and Bam glanced over the small audience for any objections.

"Yes, I do," Victoria said standing up.

"Object to what?" Bam and Desire asked in unison.

DESIRE

"Ten years ago, Bam raped me and I have been keeping it a secret. Desire, I bet you he has been telling you all sorts of horrible things about me to keep us apart. He was afraid that I would tell you," Victoria stated.

"I—" Desire began to say something but was cut off.

"I have to make sure that Bam doesn't do this to another woman ever again. I didn't deserve what he did to me. I even contracted an STD from him that ultimately made it impossible for me to have children."

The crowd was in shock. People began to talk to one another under their breath. Some people even left.

"How can you make such a harsh accusation? My brother would never ever violate a woman like that. Look at him, he doesn't need to. Besides, he wasn't raised to treat women that way," Angel said, totally appalled by Victoria's accusations.

"I'm not going to hide any longer. He raped me. I have already pressed charges against you, Bam. You belong in prison for what you did and I will see to it you stay a long time," Victoria vowed.

"Well hell, I object, too," Isis said while raising her hand in the air.

The wedding crowd gasped that she had cursed in the Lord's house.

"Desire slept with my man, Vada, and she slept with Sylvester, the pastor... sorry you're a bishop, right?" Isis asked Sylvester while pointing at him.

"I can't believe this," Angel said hysterically. "Sylvester, is this true?"

"You're going to believe a woman who is drunk?" Sylvester whispered into her ear.

"Desire even bribed the pastor-bishop-man to start her own high-class salon and spa. She walked away with an amount close to ten thousand dollars. If you don't believe me, follow the money trail. It was a wire transfer probably from church funds. You is a bad motherfucker...mister-pastor-bishop, your honor sir," Isis explained before falling on the floor.

"No, it's not true," Sylvester commented. "Those are all lies!"

"And she pregnant!" Isis said looking at Bam. "And we both know that's not your child because you's a holy man and wanted to wait for marriage before having sex and stuff. Ain't that right," Isis asked laughing.

"This is ridiculous. I have not slept with this woman," Sylvester announced.

Desire couldn't believe her friends ruined her wedding and her chance at a happy life. At that moment she wished she had never known either of them.

Just as Desire turned to look at Bam, the church doors opened. A man and a woman stepped into the church.

"Martin Winfield, AKA Bam, you are under arrest for the rape of Victoria Peterson. Before we take you into custody, we will read you your Miranda rights."

Desire, along with Bam and everyone else, turned and looked at the man and woman as they approached the altar. The best day of her life had turned into a nightmare, and once again she could not control what was happening, nor figure out a way to fix it. All she could do was cry. Suddenly she felt hot and nauseous. When the officers locked the cuffs around her husband-to-be's wrists, Desire felt dizzy and suddenly the room went black.

Angel, her mother and her father ran to Bam's side. He was led from the church with his family running behind him.

We'd like to thank you for supporting G Street Chronicles and invite you to join our social networks.
Please be sure to post a review when you're finished reading.

Like us on Facebook
G Street Chronicles
G Street Chronicles CEO Exclusive Readers Group

Follow us on Twitter
@GStreetChronicl

Follow us on Instagram
gstreetchronicles

Email us and we'll add you to our mailing list
fans@gstreetchronicles.com

George Sherman Hudson, CEO
Shawna A., COO